Diaries

Meg Cabot is the author of the phenomenally successful The Princess Diaries series. With vast numbers of copies sold around the world, the books have topped the US and UK bestseller lists for weeks and won several awards. Two movies based on the series have been massively popular throughout the world.

Meg is also the author of the bestselling Airhead trilogy, *All American Girl, All American Girl: Ready or Not, How to Be Popular, Jinx, Teen Idol, Avalon High, Tommy Sullivan Is a Freak*, The Mediator series and the Allie Finkle series as well as many other books for teenagers and adults. She and her husband divide their time between New York and Florida.

Visit Meg Cabot's website at
www.megcabot.co.uk

Books by Meg Cabot

The Princess Diaries series

The Mediator series

The Airhead trilogy

All American Girl
All American Girl: Ready or Not

Avalon High
Avalon High manga: The Merlin Prophecy
Teen Idol
How to Be Popular
Jinx
Tommy Sullivan Is a Freak
Nicola and the Viscount
Victoria and the Rogue

For younger readers
The Allie Finkle series

For older readers
The Guy Next Door
Boy Meets Girl
Every Boy's Got One
Queen of Babble series
The Heather Wells series

Also available in audio

The Princess Diaries

After Eight

Meg Cabot

GALWAY COUNTY LIBRARIES

MACMILLAN

First published in the UK 2007 by Macmillan Children's Books

This edition published 2007 by Macmillan Children's Books
a division of Macmillan Publishers Limited
20 New Wharf Road, London N1 9RR
Basingstoke and Oxford
Associated companies throughout the world
www.panmacmillan.com

ISBN 978-0-230-76801-7

Copyright © Meg Cabot LLC 2007

The right of Meg Cabot to be identified as the
author of this work has been asserted by her in accordance
with the Copyright, Designs and Patents Act 1988.

All rights reserved. No part of this publication may be
reproduced, stored in or introduced into a retrieval system, or
transmitted, in any form or by any means (electronic, mechanical,
photocopying, recording or otherwise), without the prior written
permission of the publisher. Any person who does any unauthorized
act in relation to this publication may be liable to criminal
prosecution and civil claims for damages.

1 3 5 7 9 8 6 4 2   J319.338
£9.11

A CIP catalogue record for this book is available from
the British Library.

Typeset by Intype Libra Ltd
Printed and bound by CPI Group (UK) Ltd, Croydon, CR0 4YY

This book is sold subject to the condition that it shall not,
by way of trade or otherwise, be lent, resold, hired out,
or otherwise circulated without the publisher's prior consent
in any form of binding or cover other than that in which
it is published and without a similar condition including this
condition being imposed on the subsequent purchaser.

For Abby, with love and thanks

Many thanks to Beth Ader, Jennifer Brown,
Barbara Cabot, Sarah Davies, John Henry Dreyfuss,
Michele Jaffe, Laura Langlie, Amanda Maciel,
Abigail McAden and especially Benjamin Egnatz.

'I suppose' – to Sara – 'that you feel now that you are a princess again.'

'I tried not to be anything else,' she answered in a low voice. 'Even when I was coldest and hungriest. I tried *not* to be.'

A Little Princess
Frances Hodgson Burnett

ME, A PRINCESS???? YEAH, RIGHT
A Screenplay by
Mia Thermopolis
(first draft)

Scene 12

INT/DAY – The Palm Court at the Plaza Hotel in New York City. A flat-chested girl with upside-down-Yield-sign-shaped hair (fourteen-year-old MIA THERMOPOLIS) is sitting at an ornately set table across from a bald man (her father, PRINCE PHILIPPE). We can tell by MIA's expression that her father is telling her something upsetting.

>   PRINCE PHILIPPE
> You're not Mia Thermopolis any more,
> honey.

>   MIA
> (blinking with astonishment)
> I'm not? Then who am I?

>   PRINCE PHILIPPE
> You're Amelia Mignonette Grimaldi
> Thermopolis Renaldo, Princess of
> Genovia.

Tuesday, September 7, Intro to Creative Writing

Oh, she has GOT to be kidding. Describe a room? *That* is our first assignment? DESCRIBE A ROOM? Does she have any idea how long I've been describing rooms creatively? I mean, I've described rooms in SPACE – for instance, in my *Battlestar Galactica* fan fic about Starbuck and Apollo finally Doing It.

You know what I can't believe? I can't believe she stuck me in Intro to Creative Writing. I should be in Intermediate at least. I mean, with my practice PSAT scores – which, OK, were about as low as they could be in math, but were GREAT in verbal – I should have tested into it.

And OK, the SATs don't measure creativity (unless we're supposed to believe that those people grading the essay part really read them).

But my verbal score alone should prove that I'm capable of describing a ROOM. Doesn't she know I've moved on from describing rooms – and even from writing novels – to writing whole screenplays?

Because Lilly is totally right, there's no other way I'm ever going to get a true representation of the story of my life on to the silver screen unless I write it myself. And Lilly directs it. I know it's going to be tricky finding financing and all, but J.P. said he'd help. And he knows TONS of people in Hollywood. Just the other day he and his parents had dinner with Steven Spielberg's cousin.

Why can't Ms Martinez see that by putting me in Intro to Creative Writing instead of Intermediate, where I belong, she is repressing my artistic growth? How is the blossom of my creativity ever going to be able to bloom if no one WATERS it?

Describe a room. OK, here's a room for you, Ms Martinez:

The four stone walls press narrowly against one another, glistening with moisture dripping from the low ceiling. The only light that filters in comes from the single tiny barred window near the ceiling. The only furnishings are a narrow cot with a thin mattress made of striped ticking, and a bucket. The purpose of the bucket is made obvious by the stench emanating from it. Is that what is attracting the rats that lurk in the shadowed corners, their pink noses quivering?

C-

Mia, when I said describe a room, I meant describe a room you know well. While I'm certain dungeons like the one you're describing do exist in your palace in Genovia, I highly doubt you've spent much time there. Furthermore, I happen to know from my membership of Amnesty International that Genovia is not on the watch list for inhuman treatment of prisoners, which leads to my next question: When was the last time the dungeons in your palace were even used? And I believe a man as forward-thinking as your father would have installed a proper sewage system in the palace by now, making the need for buckets for human waste obsolete.

L. Martinez

Tuesday, September 7, English

MIA!!!! Aren't you EXCITED???? It's a whole new school year! We're JUNIORS!!! JUST ONE YEAR AWAY FROM RULING THE SCHOOL!!!! Oh, your hair looks great by the way - T

Do you really think so, Tina? About my hair? Mom and I took Rocky to Astor Place Hairstylists yesterday for his first haircut, since it was the only place open, seeing as how it was Labor Day. He wouldn't stop screaming bloody murder about it, so I volunteered to let them trim mine first, to show him it didn't hurt. I have to admit, I was kind of startled when they got the clippers out!

I think it's great. You look just like Audrey Hepburn in Roman Holiday! What did Michael say when he saw it????

I haven't seen him since I got back from Genovia. We're meeting at Number One Noodle Son tonight though. I can't WAIT!!! He says he has something VERY IMPORTANT he needs to tell me, that he can't tell me over the phone or IM.

What do you think it is???? And Number One Noodle Son? That's a little out of his neighbour-hood, isn't it? Hasn't he moved into the dorm yet?

No, not yet. Something about his housing. I think that's what he wants to tell me. Maybe he's getting his own apartment or something.

OH MY GOD!!! Can you imagine, if he had his own place???? No room-mates to burst in on you. And his own kitchen!!! He could make you romantic dinners!!!!!

I don't KNOW if that's what it is. He was very vague about it on the phone.

He'd better be getting his own place. What does he think, you're going to make out at his parents' place, in front of Lilly . . . not to mention his MOM?????

Ha. Although Michael's mom probably wouldn't even notice, she spends so much time up at his dad's apartment.

Are the Drs Moscovitz getting back together???

I hope so! Michael says they've started 'dating'. Each other!

Well, that's better than if they were dating other people, I guess. Still, they might as well just get back together, in that case. Save money on rent. God, I'm glad my parents just ignore each other, like a normal couple.

Totally. Speaking of hair, what do you think of Lilly's highlights?

She says J.P. prefers blondes. I don't know. I never thought LILLY would be someone who'd change how she looks for a GUY. J.P. must be a total sexual dynamo.

TINA!!!! They haven't Done It!!!!!

Oh. I just assumed.

OH MY GOD, WHY????

Well, he DID go to her place in Albany that weekend.

Whatever, that was just because his parents were checking out some summer stock companies upstate! If they'd Done It, she'd have told us. I mean, don't you think she'd have told us?

She'd have told you, maybe. She'd never tell ME. Lilly thinks I'm a goody-two-shoes.

She does not!!!!

Yes, she does. But that's OK. I AM a goody-two-shoes. I mean, I don't even want to SEE It. Let alone Touch It. Could you imagine having one? I'd die. Do you think Lilly's touched J.P.'s?

NO WAY!!!! She'd have told me. I mean, it's true I haven't seen her since I got back from Genovia for the summer. But still. She'd have told me if she'd . . . you know. At least I *think* so . . .

She touched Boris's.

WHAT????? Also AAAAAAAAAAAAAHHHHHHHH-
HHHHHHH!!! WHY DID YOU TELL ME
THAT??????

Well, I didn't want to know either!!!! Boris told
me!!!!

WHY DID HE TELL *YOU* THAT????

Because of that book my aunt gave me - you know,
Your Precious Gift.

Oh, right. That one about how your virginity is a
precious gift you should only give to the person
you marry, because you can only give it once, and you
don't want to give it to someone who won't value it.

Yeah. Only the book doesn't say anything about what
you're supposed to do if after you marry the person you find out that he's gay, something you might
have known before you went to all the expense of a
wedding if you hadn't waited. But whatever. Boris
saw the book on my shelf and was worried I might
be upset that Lilly had touched it before I did. Even
though he's still, you know. A virgin. It was just
touching.

Did she touch it OVER or UNDER the pants?

Under.

I'm sorry, Tina. I know Boris is your boyfriend. But I am totally going to throw up now.

I know. Let's face it, Mia. You and I are going to be the Last Virgins at Albert Einstein High.

Wow. That sounds like the title of a book.

You should totally write it!!!! THE LAST VIRGINS.

– Two girls cursed with Israeli-trained bodyguards, paid by their fathers to protect their daughters' Precious Gifts . . . with their *lives*!

No man shall know them – UNTIL PROM NIGHT!!!!

Oops, Sperry's looking this way. I guess we should pay attention. Do you have any idea what she's talking about?

Who cares? This is way more interesting.

Totally. So . . . you really think she's touched J.P.'s too?

I already told you! I think they full on Did It!

No. She'd have told me. Don't you think she'd have told me?

You're the one who's known her since first grade or

8

whatever. Only you would know the answer to that. But she IS blonde now.

Hey! I'm blonde! And I still have my Precious Gift!

Oh yeah. Sorry. I forgot.

Tuesday, September 7, French

I can't believe Tina thinks Lilly and J.P. Did It over the summer. That is just ridiculous. Lilly would TOTALLY have told me if she had given away her Precious Gift.

Wouldn't she?

Besides, J.P. still hasn't even said the L word to her. Would Lilly really have sex for the first time with someone who hasn't even admitted he loves her? I mean, she's told him she loves him like nine million times, and all he ever says is *Thank You*. Or sometimes *I Know*.

But Lilly thinks that's just his way of paying homage to Han Solo.

It's pretty obvious J.P. has intimacy issues. I mean, he and Lilly have been going out for six months now. And he still doesn't even refer to her as his girlfriend. He just calls her Moscovitz.

Michael used to call me Thermopolis. But that was BEFORE we started going out.

Would Lilly have sex with someone who calls her Moscovitz and introduces her to people as his 'friend' and not his 'girlfriend'?

No way. Not Lilly.

Although she *did* go blonde. She SAYS it's because one of the producers who optioned her TV show told her that having light hair around her face makes her features look less irregular.

But it's no secret that J.P. likes blondes. I mean, Keira Knightley is like his dream girl. He's the only guy I know who sat through *Pride and Prejudice* as many times as Lilly and Tina and I did. I thought it was just because he admired the screen adaptation, but later he even admitted it was because he admired a certain tall skinny blonde (which is weird because Keira wasn't even blonde in that movie).

Poor Lilly. She can lose weight and dye her hair, but she'll never STRETCH. At least, not to be five seven, like Keira.

Hey, I wonder if THAT's what Michael wants to talk to me about tonight at dinner . . . that he found out Lilly and J.P. Did It!

God, that BETTER not be it. If Lilly Did It and she told Michael, I will never freaking hear the end of it.

Oh, great. We're supposed to *décrire un soir amusant avec les amis* in 200 words.

Un autre soir palpitant, et mes camarades et moi nous nous sommes installés devant la télé. Les choix ont paru interminables, les chaines, sans fin. Avec le cable, n'importe quoi a été possible. Et qu'est-ce que nous avons vu? La chaine des nouvelles? La chaine des sports? La chaine des 'rock-vidéos'? Non – la chaine douze. Oui! La chaine religieuse et ridicule

61 words. 139 to go.

I passed Lana in the hallway on the way to this class. She hasn't changed a bit over summer break, except, if possible, to get snottier.

Oh, and she seems to have acquired a tiny clone, some Lana wannabe, who looks exactly like her but is just a little shorter.

Anyway, as I went by, Lana looked at my head, elbowed her clone, and started laughing.

'Look, it's Peter Pan!' she yelled, for everyone in the hallway to hear.

It's good to know that however Lana spent her summer she managed to retain the charm and wit she is so widely known for throughout Albert Einstein High.

Do I really look like Peter Pan with this haircut?

Est-ce vraiment que je ressemble à Peter Pan dans cette coupe de cheveux?

Tuesday, September 7, Lunch

TOTALLY grabbed Lilly by the taco bar and asked her if she and J.P. Did It over the summer.

Her very unsatisfactory answer: 'Do you really think if I did I'd tell YOU, Bigmouth Bass?'

I have to admit, this hurt. I have faithfully kept every secret she ever told me. I never told about the time she snuck her mother's copy of *The Happy Hooker* out of the apartment and brought it to school in the fifth grade, and read the sex parts out loud to us at recess, did I?

And what about that time she told Norman, her stalker, that if he got her tickets to see *Avenue Q* she'd send him her Steve Madden platform flip-flops, and Norman got her the tickets but she never sent him the shoes, because she's never even owned a pair of Steve Madden platform flip-flops?

And I never told anyone how Lilly threw my Strawberry Shortcake doll on the roof of her parents' country house and I never saw it again until the next summer when Michael was cleaning out the gutters and he threw it down into the yard and poor Strawberry's eyes had been chewed out by squirrels and her hair was all mouldy and her face had been melted by the sun into a silent scream, even though the sight of it emotionally scarred me for life. I really loved that doll.

But I didn't want Lilly to see how much her comment hurt me, so I just shrugged and said, 'Whatever. I know you touched Boris you-know-where. He told Tina.'

But Lilly, instead of gagging, as would have been the proper response, just looked up at the ceiling and said, 'You are so juvenile.'

'Seriously, Lilly.' I couldn't help but let a little of the

hurt I felt creep into my voice. 'I can't believe you didn't tell me.'

'Because it was no big deal,' Lilly said.

'No big deal? You TOUCHED one.'

'Do we really have to discuss this in the middle of the caff?' Lilly wanted to know.

'Well, where else are we going to discuss it? Back at the lunch table, in front of your BOYFRIEND?'

'All right,' Lilly said, turning back to the taco bar. 'So I touched one. What do you want to know about it?'

I couldn't believe we were having this discussion over vats of sour cream and shredded cheddar cheese. But it was Lilly's fault. She couldn't have brought it up at one of our slumber parties, like a normal girl. Oh no, not Lilly. She had to keep it this giant secret, until BORIS, of all people, spilt the beans.

The thing is, even though it was totally embarrassing and sort of gross and all . . . I really wanted to know.

I know. It's sick. But I did.

'Well,' I said. Fortunately there was no one else around, as everyone seemed to be going for the stir fry. 'For starters, what did it feel like?'

Lilly just shrugged. 'Skin.'

I stared at her. 'That's all? Just . . . *skin*?'

'Um, that's what it's made out of,' Lilly said. 'What would you expect it to feel like?'

'I don't know,' I said. It's kind of hard to judge these things through layers of denim. Especially button-fly. That is a lot of rivets. 'In Tina's romance novels they always say it feels like molten satin over a steel rod of desire.'

Lilly considered this. Then she shrugged again and went, 'Well, yeah. That too.'

14

'OK,' I said. 'I'm officially going to throw up.'

'Well, don't do it in the guacamole. Will you go away now?'

'No,' I said. 'What does Michael want to talk to me about at Number One Noodle Son?'

'Probably,' Lilly said, 'that he wants you to Touch It.'

When I lifted the serving spoon from the sour cream and aimed it at her, she shrieked and said, laughing, 'Seriously, I don't know. I've barely seen him this summer, he's been so busy with his stupid electrical engineering project.'

So I put the spoon down. I knew she was telling the truth. Michael had been busy with his Advanced Topics in Control Theory course, which, he explained to me when I asked what the heck that meant, was all about robots. His final project for the class had been a robotic arm that could be used to help perform closed-chest, beating heart surgery. 'The ultimate goal,' Michael had said, 'in the robotic surgery field.'

Yes. I have a boyfriend who builds robots. It's SO COOL!!!!!

When Lilly and I got back to the table, it was really hard for me even to look at Boris's face – although it's actually semi-attractive now that he no longer wears a bionator and has started seeing a dermatologist and got Lasik eye surgery and all that.

Still. All I can see when I look at him now is Lilly's hand down his pants. Right there with his sweater (which he still always tucks in!).

'Oh my God, Mia,' Ling Su cried, as I sat down. 'What happened to your hair?'

This is really not the kind of thing you want to hear when you've just got your hair cut.

15

'Astor Place Hairstylists,' I said. 'Why? You don't like it?'

'Oh no, I like it,' Ling Su said quickly. But I totally saw her exchange looks with Perin, whom, I might add, has even shorter hair than I do. And mine's pretty short.

'I think Mia looks great,' J.P. said. He was sitting down at the other end of the table, across from Lilly. He wasn't looking too bad himself, actually. His tousled blond hair had been streaked even blonder in places by the sun – his parents have a place on Martha's Vineyard, which is where he'd spent the bulk of his summer, brushing up on his windsurfing skills.

And it had totally paid off. I mean, if a killer tan and pretty well-defined arm muscles count for anything.

Not that I was looking. Because I already have a boyfriend with his own killer arm muscles.

And OK, Michael probably didn't get tan this summer, because he was too busy with his summer school robot project.

But he's still hotter than J.P.

Who, besides, is Lilly's boyfriend.

Or something.

'Very gaminesque,' J.P. said, nodding at my head.

'I know what that means,' Tina said excitedly. 'Like Audrey Hepburn in *Roman Holiday*!'

'I was thinking more Keira Knightley in *Domino*,' J.P. said. 'But that works too.'

It's nice to have such supportive friends.

Well, SOME supportive friends anyway. I can't believe Lilly won't tell me if she and J.P. Did It. If they did, you can't tell by looking at them. You'd think if they'd given each other their Precious Gift, there'd at least be some footsies under the table.

But the only thing I saw them do that was at all intimate was J.P. giving Lilly a bite of his Yodel. And *I've* given her bites of my Yodel.

But that doesn't mean I'm about to give her my Precious Gift.

Tuesday, September 7, Gifted and Talented

OK, it really isn't fair that besides the whole being put in Intro to Creative Writing and not Intermediate Creative Writing, I should also have such a sucky afternoon schedule. Look at this. Just LOOK:

Period 1   Homeroom
Period 2   Intro to Creative Writing
Period 3   English
Period 4   French

Lunch

Period 5   G and T
Period 6   PE
Period 7   Chemistry
Period 8   Pre-Calculus

Physical education, then CHEMISTRY, then PRE-CALCULUS??? Is it too much to ask that I have ONE FUN CLASS in the afternoon? ONE THING TO LOOK FORWARD TO???

But no. It has to be SUCKZONE from 1.25 p.m. on.

Seriously. That is just wrong.

And who do they think they're kidding, putting me in Advanced Algebra? ME?

Whatever. Considering how bad my practice PSAT math score was, maybe I can talk Dad out of making me go to Princess Lessons this year and have mandatory tutoring instead.

AND MICHAEL COULD BE MY TUTOR!!!!

Hey, it could happen. He tutored me all through Algebra and Geometry. And I passed both of those. Why shouldn't Dad also hire him to be my tutor for Pre-Calculus?

And maybe he could tutor me in Chemistry too. Because I heard that class is no joke.

Oh, great. Lilly wants to talk about the student election. She says she's going to nominate me at assembly today.

Seriously. I just don't know. I mean, she's got our platform all set up and everything. All I have to do is run.

But I barely had a minute to myself last year! And if I really want to be a novelist – or a screenwriter or even a SHORT STORY writer or whatever – I HAVE to have some time to myself in order to ACTUALLY WRITE SOMETHING. I mean, besides my journal and *Battlestar Galactica* fan fics.

And then there's Michael. I barely got to see him last year, we were both so busy with school. On top of which I also had princess stuff to do, not to mention a new baby brother. Something's got to give this year.

And I'm thinking it's going to be student government.

Why can't LILLY run for president? I mean, I know she thinks everybody hates her, but that's just not true. I'm sure they've all forgotten about how she tried to convince the trustees to make the day an extra period longer so we could squeeze in a mandatory Latin class.

How am I going to break it to her that I don't want to run though? Especially when she's already got seventy-five *Vote for Mia* T-shirts printed up, and is looking into leasing the school roof to cell tower distributors and using the extra income to provide free laptops to the school's scholarship students?

Man. Being responsible blows.

Tuesday, September 7, Chemistry

Wow. Kenny Showalter is in this class. Is it impossible for me to take a science class in this school and NOT have Kenny Showalter be in it?

Apparently so.

Somehow he got even TALLER over the summer. He's as tall as Lars now.

Unfortunately for him, however, I think he still weighs less than I do.

He just sat down next to me. I wonder if he'll want to be lab partners again. This wouldn't be the worst thing, since if he hadn't been lab partners with me last year in Earth Science, I'd have flunked. Or at least got much worse than a C.

Hey! J.P. just walked in. J.P. is in this class too!

Thank God. At least there's ONE normal person I can ask what's going on. I mean, Kenny is great and all, but, you know. There's always that TENSION between us, because of his dumping me for thinking I was in love with Boris Pelkowski. God, that was so long ago! You'd think we'd both be over that by now, but it's still there, this little bit of tension between us when he's doing my homework for me.

I just waved for J.P. to sit on my other side, which he very nicely did. God, he is so great. I'm SO glad Lilly is going out with him. I have to admit, I didn't have much faith in her taste in guys for a while there, what with Jangbu and Franco and all. But she's really redeemed herself with—

Whoa. Kenny just passed me a note.

Mia – I didn't know you were taking Chemistry this year. Want to be lab partners again? I mean, why break with tradition? ☺

WHY WOULD KENNY WANT TO BE LAB PART-NERS WITH ME???? I mean, apart from the fact that I have better handwriting than he does, I can see no possible advantage for him in being lab partners with me. It's true he doesn't know how bad my math practice PSAT score was.

But he KNOWS I suck in science. I can only bring our group effort down! J319.338

Oh, wait. Now J.P. just passed me a note.

Hey, Mia. I didn't know you had Chem with Hipskin this semester. He's supposed to be good. Want to be lab partners? I suppose that's what Showalter just asked you in that note he flipped over to you. Ditch him, he'll just hold you back with his constant protestations of l'amour. I'm the one you want.

GALWAY COUNTY LIBRARIES

Which is funny, but – Oh dear. What do I do? I WANT to be lab partners with J.P., because I really like J.P. He is very amusing and besides which gets straight As – except for in Honours English last year, since he ALSO had Ms Martinez (only for a different class period than mine) and she gave him a B same as me because – we decided – she just didn't like our writing style.

But Kenny asked first. And Kenny and I are ALWAYS partners. He's right, we can't break with tradition.

WHY DO THESE THINGS ALWAYS HAPPEN TO ME????

Wait, I can figure this out. I mean, I haven't had TWO YEARS of instruction in diplomacy for nothing.

I know . . . let's all THREE be lab partners.
OK? – Mia

To which Kenny replied:

Cool! I like your new haircut, by the way. You look just like Anakin Skywalker from *The Phantom Menace*. You know, the one where he pod-races?

Great. I look like a nine-year-old boy.
J.P. just wrote:

Skilfully done, grasshopper. I see your sensei has taught you well.

Sensei! That's the first time I've ever heard anyone refer to my grandmother as THAT.

GALWAY COUNTY LIBRARIES

Would she be offended if she knew?

Are you kidding? I can totally see her in one of those karate uniforms, with a big stick, telling me that 'some lessons can't be taught. They must be lived to be understood'.

A la Terence Stamp in *Elektra*. Nice. Only it's called a gi.

What is?

22

Karate uniforms. Don't you know the ways of the fighting arts?

Sorry. But I know how to pour a formal tea.

Well, obviously you're set for life then.

Hee. It's fun talking to J.P. It's like talking to a girl, only better, because he's a guy. But there's no sexual tension because I know he likes Lilly.

This might actually turn out not to be so bad. I mean, except for the whole Chemistry part.

Matter

Pure substances		Mixtures	
Elements	Compounds	Homogenous	Heterogeneous

Pure substance – constant composition
Element – composed of single atom
Compound – two or more elements in a specific ratio
Mixture – combinations of pure substances

Only six hours until I get to see Michael. Please, God, don't let me die of boredom before then.

Tuesday, September 7, Pre-Calculus

Differentiation – finding the derivative
Derivative = slope
Derivative also rate

Integration

>   Infinite series
>   Divergent series
>   Convergent series

Wait.
  OK.
  What?

They have GOT to be kidding.

Only five hours until I see Michael.

Tuesday, September 7, Assembly

OK, well, THAT was lame. Only one person was nominated for student council president:

Me.

I am apparently running unopposed.

Principal Gupta is way disappointed in us. You can tell.

I guess I am too. I mean, I knew our school was apathetic, and all. Look how everyone rushed out and bought Diddy's new album when they KNOW he is withholding information about Biggie Small's murder from the Los Angeles Police.

But this is ridiculous.

Lilly practically cried. I guess it's not really a victory if there's no one to beat. I tried to tell her it was because we did such a great job last year, people figured there was no point in running against us, because we would just win anyway.

But then Lilly pointed out that everyone was just text messaging one another about what they're doing after school during the entire assembly, not even paying attention, so it was likely they didn't even know WHAT was going on. They probably thought it was just another convocation on daring to keep off drugs.

Homework

Homeroom: N/A
Intro to Creative Writing: Describe a scene out of your window
English: *Franny and Zooey*
French: Finish *décrire un soir amusant avec les amis*

25

G and T: Prepare a summary for Mrs Hill of what you hope to accomplish in G and T this semester.
PE: Wash gym shorts.
Chemistry: Ask Kenny/J.P.
Pre-Calculus: Seriously. This class HAS to be a joke.

ME, A PRINCESS???? YEAH, RIGHT
A Screenplay by
Mia Thermopolis
(first draft)

Scene 13

INT/DAY – The Palm Court at the Plaza Hotel in New York City. Close up of MIA's face as she tries to digest what her father, PRINCE PHILIPPE, has just told her.

> MIA
> (fighting tears. And hiccups)
> I am NOT moving to Genovia.

> PRINCE PHILIPPE
> (using his Now-Let's-Be-Reasonable voice)
> But, Mia. I thought you understood—

> MIA
> All I understand is that you *lied*
> to me my whole life. Why should I
> come live with *you*?

MIA leaps up from the table, knocking over her chair, then rushes from the restaurant, nearly knocking over the snobby doorman on her way out.

Tuesday, September 7, W Hotel

So they're converting the Plaza into condominiums and luxury timeshares. And Grandmere's already bought the penthouse.

But they're still renovating it. And Grandmere can't live there with all the dust because of her sinuses. Not to mention the banging, which starts promptly at 7.30 a.m.

So she's taken up residence at the W Hotel.

And she doesn't seem to be liking it very much.

'This,' Grandmere was saying as I walked into her suite – which, can I just say, is pretty freaking nice? I mean, it's not exactly her style (it's more modern than frou-frou – stripes and leather as opposed to floral and lace), but it's got views all up and down the island of Manhattan, and a lot of shiny wood – 'is completely unacceptable.'

She was saying this to this guy in a suit with a little gold name tag that said Robert on it.

Robert looked like he wanted to kill himself.

I sympathized. I know what Grandmere's like when she's on a tear.

And this one appeared to be a doozy.

'Daisies?' Grandmere's voice had dipped to icy registers. 'Does your staff really believe *daisies* are the appropriate flower with which to adorn the rooms of the Dowager Princess of Genovia?'

'I'm so sorry, madam,' Robert said. I saw him flick a glance over at me, all sprawled out across the kick-ass white couch in front of the flat panel TV that – yes – appears as if from nowhere when you push a button, just like Joey always wanted on *Friends*.

You could tell Robert was totally looking for a hand with the Big G.

But there was no way I was letting myself get sucked into this one. I bent over my screenplay, scribbling away very busily. J.P. says when I finish it he knows a producer who would be very interested in seeing it. Very interested! That practically means it's sold.

'We put Gerber daisies in all our rooms,' Robert went on, seeing he was getting no help from me. 'No one has ever complained about them before.'

Grandmere looked at him as if he had just said that no one had ever pulled out a knife and committed hara-kiri right in front of him before, either.

'Have you ever had a PRINCESS stay in this hotel before?' she demanded.

'Actually, the Princess of Thailand was here just last week before settling into her dorm room at NYU,' Robert began.

I winced. Wrong answer, Robert! Too bad. Thanks for playing.

'THAILAND?' Grandmere just glared at him. 'Have you any idea HOW MANY PRINCESSES OF THAILAND THERE ARE?'

Robert looked panicky. He knew he'd messed up. He just didn't know how. Poor guy. 'Um . . . no?'

'Dozens. You could even say hundreds. Do you know how many Dowager Princesses of Genovia there are, young man?'

'Um.' Robert looked like he wanted to jump out the window. I didn't blame him really. 'One?'

'One. That is correct,' Grandmere said. 'Don't you think that if the ONE DOWAGER PRINCESS OF GENOVIA demands roses in her room – pink and white roses. NOT orange Gerber daisies, which might be the trendy flower of the moment, but ROSES never go out of style – you ought to SUPPLY THEM FOR HER? Especially considering the fact that her dog happens to be allergic to *grassland plants*?'

Everyone's gaze went to Rommel, who, far from looking as if he were suffering from any sort of allergic reaction to anything, was snoring away in his gilt-frame dog bed, twitching a little as he dreamed of whatever it is dogs dream about – in Rommel's case, no doubt of running away from his owner.

'As if,' Grandmere added, 'it isn't bad enough you have actual grass GROWING in your lobby.'

Ouch. I'd noticed that as I'd come in. It's a bit *modern*, having grass growing in your lobby. I mean, for Grandmere's taste, anyway. She prefers mints in little crystal bowls.

'I understand, madam,' Robert said, actually giving a little bow. 'I'll – I'll have pink and white roses sent for immediately. I can't apologize enough for the oversight—'

'No,' Grandmere said, raising one drawn-on eyebrow. 'You cannot. Goodbye.'

Robert, gulping, turned and hurried from the room. Grandmere waited until he was gone before collapsing into one of the black-leather-and-chrome chairs across from my couch.

But of course those aren't the kind of chairs you can actually collapse into all that easily. Because the leather is kind of slippery.

'Amelia!' Grandmere cried as she slithered around on the seat. 'This is unconscionable!'

'I like it,' I said. I do. I think the W is cool. Everything in it is very shiny.

'You're mad,' Grandmere said. 'Did you know I ordered a Sidecar, and they delivered it in a TUMBLER?'

'So? More to enjoy.'

'Sidecars are never served in a TUMBLER, Amelia. WATER is served in a tumbler. A Sidecar is ALWAYS served in a stemmed cocktail glass. MY GOD, WHAT HAPPENED TO YOUR HAIR???'

Grandmere was suddenly sitting up very straight in her slippery black leather chair.

'Calm down,' I said. 'I just got a little trim—'

'A LITTLE TRIM??? You look like a cotton swab.'

'It'll grow back,' I said lamely. Because the truth is, I'm not planning on growing it back. I really like having short hair. You don't have to do ANYTHING to it. And when you look in the mirror, your head always looks the same. There's something comforting about that. I mean, it's TIRING seeing some new disaster erupting on your scalp every time you happen to glance at your reflection.

'How do you intend to keep your tiaras on with nothing for the combs to dig into?' Grandmere wanted to know.

Which is actually a good point. And certainly not one anyone had thought to bring up at Astor Place Hairstylists, least of all my mom, who'd said my new short hair reminded her of Demi Moore's in *G.I. Jane*, which at the time I'd taken to be a compliment.

'Velcro?' I asked carefully.

But Grandmere didn't think my joke was all that funny.

'There's not even any point in summoning Paolo,' she

GALWAY COUNTY LIBRARIES

said. 'Because it's not as if there's even anything left for him to work with.'

'It's not THAT short,' I said, lifting a hand to my head and feeling spikes. Well, on second thought, maybe it is. Oh well. 'Whatever. It's just HAIR. It will grow back. Don't we have more important things to worry about, Grandmere? I mean, in Iran, fundamentalist religious courts still routinely sentence women to death by being buried up to their necks in sand and then stoned, for crimes like adultery. Now! Things like this are happening RIGHT NOW!!!! And you're worried about my HAIR???'

Grandmere just shook her head. You never can distract her with current events. If it doesn't have to do with royalty, she just doesn't care.

'This could not have come at a worse time,' she went on, like I hadn't said anything. '*Vogue* just contacted the royal publicist, wanting an interview and photo shoot for their winter getaway issue. The article would bring Genovia to the attention of hundreds of women looking to schedule their winter vacation somewhere warm. Not to mention the fact that your father is in town for the General Assembly meeting at the UN.'

'Good!' I yelled. 'Maybe he can bring up the Iran thing at it! Do you know they've outlawed western music there too? And, while claiming their only interest in nuclear development is for civilian energy and not military use, for twenty years they've actually hidden atomic research that proves otherwise from the International Atomic Energy Agency? Who cares about winter getaways when we could all be blown up at any moment?'

'I suppose we could have you fitted for a wig,' Grandmere said. 'Though how we'll ever find one identical to your old haircut, I don't know. They don't make wigs shaped like sailboats. Perhaps we could find a longer wig and then have Paolo cut it . . .'

'Are you even listening to me?' I wanted to know. 'There are more important things to worry about right now than my hair. Do you know how much trouble we'll all be in if Iran gets a nuclear weapon? They BURY WOMEN UP TO THEIR NECKS AND STONE THEM FOR SLEEPING WITH GUYS THEY AREN'T MARRIED TO. How discriminating do you think they're going to be about who deserves to have a bomb dropped on them?'

'Maybe,' Grandmere said thoughtfully, 'we should turn you into a redhead. Oh no, that will never work. With that haircut, you'd look exactly like that boy from the cover of those *Mad* comic books your father used to read all the time when he was your age.'

Seriously. It's useless even to talk to her. Did I really think a woman with so unreasonable a prejudice against Gerber daisies was going to listen to me?

Sometimes I feel like burying HER up to her neck in sand and throwing rocks at her head.

Michael is here!!!!! To take me to Number One Noodle Son for dinner. Right now he's chatting with Mom and Mr G while I'm 'getting ready'. He hasn't seen me yet.

Or my haircut.

I know I'm being a complete baby about it. I know it looks fine. Mom keeps telling me it looks fine. Even Mr G, when I asked him, said he doesn't think I look like Peter Pan OR Anakin Skywalker.

Still. What if Michael hates it? In *Sixteen* magazine they're always going on about how boys like girls with long hair. At least, whenever they do those 'guy on the street' interviews. They show pictures of Keira Knightley with short hair and Keira Knightley with long hair to random high-school boys standing around outside convenience marts or whatever, and ask them which they prefer.

And nine times out of ten they pick Keira with the long hair.

Of course, none of those boys is ever Michael. But still.

Well, whatever. Michael is just going to have to deal.

OK, maybe a little more mousse –

I can hear him talking to Rocky now. Not that anyone can understand a word Rocky says, except Truck and Kitty and Cookie and More and No and MINE, the total extent of his vocabulary. Apparently this is normal for a child his age, and Rocky is not suffering from any sort of developmental retardation.

Still, it's not easy having a conversation with him. I find it endlessly fascinating, of course. But he's MY brother.

Listen to how patient Michael is being! Rocky is just saying, 'Truck,' over and over again, and Michael is going, 'Yes. That's a very nice truck,' in the sweetest way. He'd make such a good dad! Not that I have any intention of having children until I've finished college and joined the Peace Corps and put an end to global warming, of course.

Still, it's good to know that when I'm ready Michael will be up to the task.

Oh! I just snuck a peek at him! He looks sooo great, so tall and handsome and dark and broad-shouldered and oh! I think he just shaved and I can't believe it's been a whole MONTH since I saw him and . . .

Oh my God. My hair is shorter than his.

MY HAIR IS SHORTER THAN MY BOYFRIEND'S.

What have I done?

Tuesday, September 7, Kitchen of Number One Noodle Son

OK.

OK, I am trying to understand this.

That's why I asked Kevin Yang if I could sit here in the kitchen for a few minutes. Because I just need a little time to myself to figure this out. And there's someone in the ladies' room. Someone who apparently doesn't realize there are girls out here whose lives are falling apart and who need to pretend to wash their hands so they can figure out what to do about it.

And OK, it's kind of busy and hot and crowded back here, because Kevin's got all ninety of his cousins working, and it's the dinner rush, and everyone seems to have ordered the Peking duck. So everywhere I look, all I can see are smiling duck heads.

But at least I can catch my breath for a minute and try to understand what's going on.

I just don't get it.

Oh, not about Michael's reaction to my hair. I mean, he was *surprised* to see that it was so short.

But, like, not displeased. He said I looked cute – like Natalie Portman when she started growing her hair out again after she shaved it all off to play Evey Hammond in *V for Vendetta*.

And he gave me a big hug and a kiss. And then a BIGGER hug and a kiss when we were out in the hallway and Mom and Mr G weren't there and Lars was still putting on his shoulder holster. I got to smell Michael's neck, and I swear every synapse in my brain must have shot out a megadose of serotonin because of his pheromones, because I felt so relaxed and happy afterwards.

And I can *tell* he feels the same way about me. He held my hand the whole stroll to the restaurant, and we talked about everything that had happened since we last saw each other – Grandmere getting kicked out of the Plaza and Lilly going blonde (I didn't ask him if he thought Lilly and J.P. had Done It when J.P. came to their country house for the weekend, because I try to avoid discussions involving sex, since it only seems to remind Michael that we're not having it, and inflame his desire) and Rocky's dexterity with his Tonka truck and the Drs Moscovitz and their quasi-getting-back-together.

And when we got to the restaurant, Rosy, the hostess, sat us at our usual table by the window, and invited Lars to sit up at the bar with her, where he could watch me and the baseball game at the same time.

And we ordered my favourite, cold sesame noodles, and Michael's favourite, barbecued spare ribs, and we split a hot and sour soup and Michael had kung pao chicken and I had sautéed string beans, and then I said, 'So when are you moving into the dorm? Hasn't school started already?' And Michael said, 'I've been meaning to talk to you about that. That's what I wanted to wait to tell you in person.'

And I was like, 'Oh yeah?' thinking he was going to say something like he was getting his own apartment because he was tired of sharing a room with another guy, or maybe that he was moving in with his dad because Dr Moscovitz was so lonely. In fact, I was so confident that whatever Michael was about to say was going to be no

37

big deal that I took a giant bite of cold sesame noodles, right before he said:

'Remember that project I was working on this summer? The robotic arm?'

'The one with which doctors can perform closed-chest surgery on a beating heart?' I said, around the noodles. 'Uh-huh.'

'Well,' Michael said. 'I have some really good news: it works. At least, the prototype does. And my professor was so impressed that he told a colleague of his over at a company in Japan about it – a company that is attempting to perfect robotic surgical systems that can work unassisted by surgeons – and his colleague wants me to come to Japan and see if we can construct an actual working model for use in the operating room.'

'Wow,' I said, swallowing my noodles and going for another huge mouthful. I mean, I was pretty much starving. I hadn't had anything to eat since my three-bean salad at lunch. Oh, and some totally awesome wasabi peas in Grandmere's hotel room (which she tried and freaked out over. 'WHERE ARE THE CANDIED ALMONDS?' she screamed at that Robert guy. Poor thing.). 'So like when would you go? Some weekend or something?'

'No,' Michael said, shaking his head. 'You don't understand. It wouldn't be for just a weekend. It would be until the project is completed. My professor has arranged for me to receive full course credits, as well as a significant stipend, while I'm away.'

'So.' Man, those noodles were good. 'Like a week?'

'Mia,' Michael said. 'Just the prototype took all summer. Building an actual working model, with a console containing a real-time MRI, real-time CT scanner and real-time X-ray, could take up to a year. Or more. But it's a fantastic opportunity – one I can't turn down. Something I designed could potentially help to save thousands of lives. And I need to be there to make sure it happens.'

Wait. A year? Or MORE?

Of course I started choking on my cold sesame noodles, and Michael had to reach around the table and slap me on the back and I had to drink both my ice water and his Coke before I could breathe again.

And when I could breathe, all I seemed able to say was, 'What? WHAT?' over and over again.

And even though Michael was trying to explain – as patiently as if I was Rocky showing him my truck over and over – all I could hear inside my head was, 'Could take up to a year. Or more. But it's a fantastic opportunity – one I can't turn down. Could take up to a year. Or more. But it's a fantastic opportunity – one I can't turn down.'

Michael is moving to Japan. For a year. Or more.

He leaves Friday.

You can see why I had to excuse myself. Because in what universe does something like this make any sense? In Bizarro Universe, maybe. But not MY universe. Not the universe Michael and I share.

Or the one I used to think we shared.

Even as the words were still batting around in my mind: 'Could take up to a year. Or more. But it's a fantastic opportunity – one I can't turn down,' and I was like, 'Wow, Michael. That is so great. I'm so happy for you,' this voice in my head was going, *'Is it because of ME?'*

And then, somehow, the voice got OUTSIDE my

39

head, and before I could stuff it back, the words were coming out of my mouth: 'Is it because of ME?'

And Michael blinked and was like, 'What?'

It was a total nightmare. Because even though, inside my head, I was like, 'Shut up. Shut up. Shut up,' my mouth seemed to have a will of its own. A second later, before I could stop it, my mouth was going, 'Is it because of me? Are you moving to Japan because I did something?' And then my mouth went, 'Or DIDN'T do something?'

And I wanted to shove all the cold sesame noodles in the world into it, just to shut myself up.

But Michael was already shaking his head. 'No, of course not. Mia, don't you see? This is such an incredible opportunity. This company already has mechanical engineers working on drafts of my design. MY design. Something I made, which could change the course of modern surgery as we know it. Of course I have to be there.'

'But do they have to do it in *Japan*?' my mouth asked. 'Don't they have mechanical engineers here in Manhattan? I'm almost sure they do. I think Ling Su's dad is one!'

'Mia,' Michael explained, 'this is the most innovative and cutting-edge robotics research group in the world. They're based in Tsukuba, which is basically the Silicone Valley of Japan. That's where their labs are, their research facilities. All their equipment is there . . . everything I need to turn my prototype into a working model. I have to go there.'

'But you'll be back,' I said. My brain was starting to take control of my mouth again. Thank God. 'For like Thanksgiving and Christmas and Spring Break and all that.' Because the wheels in my mind were spinning, and I was thinking, *Well, OK, this won't be so bad. Sure, my boyfriend will be in Japan, but I'll still see him during vacations. It won't be THAT different than during the school year. And this way I'll have more time to really buckle down and maybe figure out what Mr Hipskin is talking about in Chemistry and just what the heck is going on in Pre-Calculus and maybe even study enough to do a little better on my math PSATs, and, what the heck, maybe I'll even stick with student government after all, and I'll be able to finish my screenplay AND maybe a novel . . .*

And that's when Michael reached across the table and said, 'Mia, there's sort of a time crunch with this project. If we're going to get it out on the market as soon as we possibly can, we can't take time off. So . . . no, I won't be home for Thanksgiving or Christmas. I probably won't be home until next summer, by which point we should have something we can demonstrate in an actual surgical setting.'

I heard the words coming out of his mouth. I knew he was speaking English. But just like with Mr Hipskin in Chemistry class, what Michael was saying made no sense. Next summer is a *year from now*. Basically Michael was saying he was going to be gone – not see me – for a YEAR.

And OK, sure, I could fly to Japan to see him. In my dreams. Because NO WAY am I going to be able to talk my dad into letting me take the Royal Genovian jet to *Japan*.

And no way would they let me fly commercial. All the air marshals in the world wouldn't satisfy Grandmere – let alone my dad – that commercial air traffic is safe for royals.

That's when I excused myself. That's why I'm sitting here. Because none of this makes any sense.

I don't care how good an opportunity it is.

I don't care how much money he stands to make from this, or how many thousands of lives he might save.

Why would any guy who loves his girl-friend as much as Michael claims to love me want to be apart from her for a YEAR?

And Kevin Yang is no help on this subject. He just shrugged when I asked him this, and went, 'I never understood Michael from the day he first came in here when he was ten years old. He asked for hot chilli oil for my dumplings. Like they are not spicy enough!'

And Lars, who poked his head in here a minute ago to see where I disappeared to, just went, 'Well, you know. Sometimes guys just have to do these things to prove themselves.'

To WHOM? Aren't *I* the only one who should matter? *I* don't want Michael to go to Japan for a year.

And excuse me, but it's not like he's going off to the Gobi Desert to do chin-ups and shoot at cardboard cut-outs of terrorists like Lars did when HE decided he needed to prove himself. He's just going to some computer lab in Japan!

And yes, I understand that his robotic arm thingy could save thousands of lives.

BUT WHAT ABOUT MY LIFE?

OK, this totally isn't helping.

And the sight of all these duck heads is really psychologically disturbing to me.

I mean, not as psychologically disturbing as the fact that my boyfriend is apparently moving to Japan for a year.

But almost.

I'm going back out there. I'm going to be supportive. I'm going to be happy for Michael. I'm not going to say anything about how if he really loved me, he wouldn't go. Because I can't be selfish. I have had Michael all to myself for nearly two years now. I can't hog him from the rest of the world, which really does need him and his genius.

Except . . .

EXCEPT WHAT AM I GOING TO DO IF I CAN'T SMELL HIS NECK????

I might die.

Tuesday, September 7, 10 p.m., the Loft

I shouldn't have done it.

I know I shouldn't have done it.

I don't know why I couldn't keep my mouth shut. I don't know why I couldn't make my lips say the things I wanted them to say, like, 'Michael, I am so proud of you,' and, 'This really is such a great opportunity.'

I mean, I DID say those things. Really, I did.

But then – as we were walking down that bike path by the Hudson (Lars could barely keep up, we were walking so fast . . . well, mostly because Lars was texting people on his Sidekick as we went, but whatever), because it was such a nice night and I wasn't ready to go home yet, because I wanted to squeeze every minute I could out of my last few days with him – and Michael was telling me how excited he was about moving to Japan, and how they eat noodles for breakfast there, and how the shumai you buy on the street are even better than the shumai at Sapporo East, somehow the words, 'But, Michael . . . what about US?' slipped out of my mouth before I could stuff them back in.

Which is probably the lamest, most idiotic, Lana Weinbergerish thing a girl in my position could have said. Seriously. Pretty soon I'm going to start snapping the back of my own bra and be all, 'Why are you wearing a bra, Mia? You don't need one.'

But Michael didn't even skip a beat. He went, 'I think we'll be fine. Of course I'm going to miss you. But I have to admit, it's going to be a lot easier to miss you than it's been to be around you lately.'

And I totally froze in the middle of the bike path and was like, 'WHAT?'

Because I'd *known* it. I'd totally KNOWN it. I'd asked him if part of why he was going had to do with me.

And it turned out I was right.

'It's just,' he said, 'that sometimes I'm not sure how much longer I'll be able to deal with it.'

To which I was all, 'Deal with WHAT?' Because I had NO IDEA what he was talking about.

'Being with you all the time,' he said, 'and not. You know.'

I STILL didn't get it (yes, I know I am the one who is suffering from developmental retardation and not Rocky after all).

I was like, 'Being with me all the time and not WHAT?'

And Michael finally just had to say, 'Not having sex.'

!!

!!

!!!

Yes, that's right. My boyfriend apparently doesn't mind moving to Japan so much, because that is easier than being around me and not having sex.

I guess I should consider myself fortunate, since it's clear from this that my boyfriend is a sex maniac, and I am probably lucky to be getting rid of him.

But of course that didn't occur to me at the time. At

the time, I was just so shocked by what he said that I had to sit down.

And the closest seat was a swing in the Hudson River Park playground.

So I sat down on a swing and looked down at my knees while Michael said, 'I told you last year that I'm willing to wait.' He sat down on the swing next to mine. 'And I *am* willing to wait, Mia. Although to tell you the truth I'm not really sure how you think the whole prom night thing is going to work since I am not going to your senior prom because I already graduated and my prom days are over, and it's totally lame for girls to bring their college boyfriends to the prom. But whatever. The fact remains that your senior prom isn't for two more years. And two years is a long time for us to keep – well, doing what we're doing. I'm getting really tired of taking so many cold showers.'

I TOTALLY couldn't look at him after that. I could feel my face turning bright red. Fortunately it was getting dark out so I don't think he noticed. I mean, the street lamps were starting to turn on. We were the only ones on the swings, so it wasn't like anyone could overhear us. Lars was pretending to be very interested in the view of the river a few dozen yards away – but really he was scoping on all the pretty rollerbladers – so there was no danger of him eavesdropping.

Still. It was totally *embarrassing*.

I mean, I guess I knew where Michael was coming from. I always did wonder what he did, you know, after a heavy duty make-out session, about the whole . . . well, what-was-going-on-in-his-pants issue.

Now I guess I know.

'It's just,' Michael went on, as over in the sandbox

46

some little kids ran around trying to throw sand on each other, while their mothers gossiped on a bench not far away, 'that it's not easy, Mia. I mean, it seems like it's easy for you—'

'It's not easy for me,' I interrupted. Because it's NOT easy for me. I mean, there are lots of times when I think about how great it would be to just, you know, rip his clothes off and have my way with him. I've even got to a point now where the idea of letting him rip my clothes off ME is starting to have its appeal, whereas before, the thought of him seeing me naked made my mouth go dry.

Only . . . where is this clothes-ripping-off supposed to happen? In my room, with my mom in the next room? In HIS room, with HIS mom in the next room? In his dorm room, with my bodyguard in the hallway, and his room-mate busting in at any moment?

And what about birth control? And what about the fact that once you Do It, that's ALL you want to do when you get together? I mean, goodbye *Star Wars* movie marathons. Hello, edible body paint.

Whatever, I've read *Cosmo*. I know the score.

'Right,' Michael said. 'Anyway, given all that, I just think my spending a year abroad might not be the worst idea.'

I couldn't believe it had come to this. Seriously. Suddenly I just – well, I couldn't stop myself. I started crying.

And I couldn't stop.

Which was HORRIBLE of me, because OF COURSE his going was a GOOD THING. I mean, if his robot arm thingy could really do everything all these people were thinking it could do – if Columbia University was willing to let him go off to Japan and work for some company and get course credit while doing so – well, crying about it wasn't a very princessy thing for me to do, was it?

But I never said I was very good at being princessy.

'Mia,' Michael said, coming off his swing and kneeling in the sand in front of me, and taking my hands in his. He was sort of laughing. I guess I'd be laughing too, if some girl was crying as hard as I was. Seriously. It was like I was one of those little kids in the sandbox, who'd fallen down and skinned their knee. The moms over on the bench even looked at me in alarm, thinking the sound was coming from one of their kids. When they saw it was just me, they started whispering together – probably because they recognized me from *Inside Edition* ('Princess Mia of Genovia's romantic life took another tumble the other night, as longtime boyfriend, Columbia student Michael Moscovitz, announced he was moving to Japan, and the princess responded by crying on a park swing').

'This is a *good* thing, Mia,' Michael said. 'Not just for me, but for *us*. It's my chance to prove to your grandmother and all those people who think I'm a big nobody and not good enough for you that I actually *am* somebody, and might possibly even be worthy of you someday.'

'You're *totally* worthy of me,' I wailed. The truth is, of course, I'm not worthy of *him*. But I didn't say that out loud.

'A lot of people don't think so,' Michael said.

And I couldn't exactly say that wasn't true, because he's right. It seems like every other week *Us Weekly* runs some article about who I should be dating instead of Michael. Prince William was high on the list last week, but Wilmer Valderrama usually makes a token appearance every other month or so. There'll be a picture of

Michael coming out of class or something, next to a picture of James Franco or whoever, and then they'll put like a two per cent over Michael's picture to show that only two per cent of the readers polled think I should be with Michael, and then a ninety-eight per cent over James Franco, showing that everyone else thinks I should be with some guy who never did anything in his life except stand in front of a camera and say a bunch of words somebody else wrote, and then maybe have a sword-fight that was choreographed for him.

And of course my grandmother's feelings on the matter are so well known they are almost legendary.

'The fact is, Mia,' Michael said, his dark eyes looking very intently up into my not dark ones. 'As much as you might like to pretend it isn't true, you're a princess. You're going to be a princess *forever*. You're going to rule a country someday. You already know what your destiny is. It's all laid out for you. I don't have that. I still have to figure out who I am and how I'm going to leave my mark on the world. And if I'm going to be with you, it's going to have to be a pretty big mark, because everyone thinks a guy has to be pretty special in order to be with a princess. I'm just trying to live up to everyone's expectations.'

'*My* expectations should be the only ones that matter,' I said.

'They're the ones that matter most,' Michael said, squeezing my hands. 'Mia, you know I'd never be happy just being your consort – walking one step behind you all the time. And I know you'd never be happy if that's all I was either.'

I winced at the reminder of the Genovian Parliament's hideous rules for whoever I marry – my so-called consort, who will have to rise the moment I rise, not lift his fork until I've lifted mine, not engage in any sort of risk-taking behaviour (such as racing, either car or boat, mountain-climbing, sky-diving, et cetera) until such time as an heir has been provided; give up his right, in the event of annulment or divorce, to custody of any children born during the marriage . . . and also give up the citizenship of his native country in favour of citizenship of Genovia.

'It's not that I wouldn't be willing to do any of that stuff,' Michael went on. 'I'd be fine with it if I knew that . . . well, that I'd accomplished something with my life too . . . not ruling a country, maybe. But something like . . . well, something like I have the opportunity to do now. Make a difference. The way *you'll* be making a difference some day.'

I blinked down at him. It wasn't that I didn't understand. I *did* understand. Michael was right. He isn't the kind of guy who could be happy walking one step behind me all his life – unless he had his own thing. Whatever that thing was.

I just didn't understand why his own thing had to be all the way in JAPAN.

'Listen,' Michael said, squeezing my hands again. 'You'd better quit crying. Lars looks like he's ready to come over.'

'That's his job,' I pointed out, sniffling. 'He's supposed to protect me from . . . from . . . getting hurt!'

And the realization that this was a hurt not even a six-foot-five guy with a gun could protect me from just made me sniffle harder.

What was even more infuriating was that Michael just started laughing.

'It's not *funny*,' I sniffled through my tears.

'It sort of is,' Michael said. 'I mean, you have to admit. We're a pretty pathetic pair.'

'I'll tell you what's pathetic,' I said. 'You're going to go away to Japan and meet some geisha girl and forget all about me. *That's* what's pathetic.'

'What would I want with some geisha girl,' Michael wanted to know, 'when I could have you?'

'Geisha girls have sex with you whenever you want,' I pointed out between sniffles. 'I know, I saw that movie.'

'Well,' Michael said. 'Actually, now that you mention it, a geisha girl might not be so bad.'

So then I had to hit him. Even though I still wasn't seeing anything funny in the situation.

I still don't. It's a horrible, unfair, completely tragic situation.

Oh sure, I stopped crying. And when Lars came over and asked if everything was all right, I told him it was.

But it wasn't.

And it isn't. Everything will never be all right again.

But I acted like I was OK with it. I mean, I had to, right? I let Michael walk me home, and I even held his hand the whole way. And at the door to the loft, I let him kiss me, while Lars politely pretended to need to tie his shoe at the bottom of the stairs. Which was good because there was also some under-the-bra action going on.

But in a tender way, like in that scene where Jennifer Beals and Michael Nouri are in the abandoned factory in *Flashdance*.

And when Michael whispered, 'Are we OK?' I said, 'Yes, we're OK,' even though I don't believe we are. At least, *I'm* not.

And when Michael said, 'I'll call you tomorrow,' I said, 'You do that.'

And then I went inside the loft, walked straight to the fridge, took out the container of macadamia brittle Häagen-Dazs, grabbed a spoon, went into my room and ate the whole thing.

But I still don't feel OK.

I don't think I'll ever feel OK again.

Tuesday, September 7, 11 p.m.

My mom just tapped on my door and was all, 'Mia? Are you in there?'

I said I was, and she opened the door.

'I didn't even hear you come in,' she said. 'Did you have a nice time with—'

Then her voice trailed off, because she'd seen the empty Häagen-Dazs container. And my face.

'Honey,' she said, sinking down on to the bed beside me. 'What happened?'

And all of a sudden, I started crying all over again, like I hadn't just been crying an hour before.

'He's moving to Japan,' was all I could say. And I flung myself into her arms.

I wanted to tell her a lot more. I wanted to tell her about how it was all my fault, for not sleeping with him (even though I know, deep down inside, that's not really true). It's more my fault because I'm a princess – a freaking PRINCESS – and what guy could live up to that, EVER? Except a prince.

The worst part is, being a princess isn't even something I DID. I mean, it's not like I saved the President from being shot like Samantha Madison, or found all those missing kids with my psychic powers like Jessica Mastriani, or kept a hundred tourists from drowning like ten-year-old Tilly Smith did when she was on that beach in Thailand and realized a tsunami was coming because she'd just been studying tsunamis in school, and told all those people to 'RUN!'

All I did was get born.

And EVERYONE has done that.

But I couldn't tell Mom any of that stuff. Because

we've been through the princess thing before. It's like Michael said: I'm a princess. I'm going to be one forever. No use complaining about it. It just IS.

So instead I just cried.

It made me feel a little better, I guess. I mean, it's always nice to get hugged by your mom, no matter how old you get. Moms don't give off pheromones – at least, I don't think they do – but they still smell really nice. At least mine does. Like Dove soap and turpentine and coffee. Which mixed together are the second-best smell in the world.

The first being Michael's neck, of course.

My mom said all the usual mom things, like, 'Oh, honey, it will be OK,' and, 'A year will go by before you know it,' and, 'If Philippe gets you the new Powerbook with the camera built in, you and Michael can videophone, and it will be like he's right in the room with you.'

Except that it won't. Because I won't be able to smell him.

But when Mr G came in to see what all the noise was about, I finally pulled myself together, and said I felt better, and not to worry about me. I tried to smile all bravely, and Mom patted me on the head and said that if I'd survived spending so much time with Grandmere, I'd survive this, easy.

But she's wrong. Spending time with Grandmere is like eating an entire container of macadamia brittle compared to being without Michael for an entire year.

Or more.

ME, A PRINCESS???? YEAH, RIGHT
A Screenplay by
Mia Thermopolis
(first draft)

Scene 2

INT/NIGHT – The penguin tank at the Central Park Zoo. In the blue glow from the water of the illuminated penguin tank, a young girl (MIA) sits alone, frantically writing in her journal.

MIA

(voiceover)

I don't know where to go or to whom to turn.
I can't go to Lilly's. She is vehemently
opposed to any form of government that is not
for the people, by the people. She's always
said that when sovereignty is vested in a
single person whose right to rule is hereditary,
the principles of social equality and respect
for the right of the individual within a
community are irrevocably lost. This is why
today, real power has passed from reigning
monarchs to constitutional assemblies, making
royals such as Queen Elizabeth mere symbols
of national unity.

Except in Genovia, apparently.

Wednesday, September 8, Homeroom

Michael told Lilly. I know he told her because when we stopped by the Moscovitzes' apartment building to pick her up for school this morning, he was standing outside with her, holding a large hot chocolate (with whipped cream) from Starbucks for me. When the limo pulled up and Hans opened the door, Michael leaned in and said, 'Good morning. This is for you. Tell me you didn't change your mind overnight and that you don't hate me now.'

Except of course I could never hate Michael. Especially when the sun is just coming up all shiny and new and its rays hit his freshly shaved neck, and when I lean over to take the hot chocolate and give him a good-morning kiss I smell his Michaely scent, which always seems to make everything seem like it's going to be OK.

Until he's out of range for me to smell him any more, anyway.

Which is definitely what he's going to be when he's in Japan.

'I don't hate you,' I said.

'Good,' he said. 'What are you doing tonight?'

'Um,' I said. 'Something with you?'

'Good answer. I'll pick you up at seven.'

Then he kissed me and got out of the way so that Lilly could get in the car. Which she did with a crabby, 'God, *move*, you *ass*,' to her brother, since she's not exactly a morning person.

Then Michael said, 'Play nice with the other kids, girls,' and shut the door. And Lilly turned to me and said, 'He's such an *ass*.'

'He totally moved when you asked him to,' I pointed out.

'Not because of *that*,' Lilly said fiercely. 'Because of this stupid Japan thing.'

'If his model works, he'll end up saving thousands of lives and making millions of dollars,' I said. My hot chocolate was too hot to sip so I blew on it. Only the whipped cream was in the way.

Lilly looked at me, her eyes all big. 'Oh my God,' she said. 'Are you going to be *reasonable* about this?'

'I don't have a choice,' I said. 'Do I?'

'I bet if you threw a big enough fit,' Lilly said, 'he wouldn't go.'

'I already did,' I assured her. 'There was crying and snot and everything. It didn't change his mind.'

Lilly just grunted upon hearing this.

'The thing is,' I said. Because I had given this a lot of thought. Like all night long. 'He has to go. I don't want him to, but it's like a thing with him. He feels like he has to prove himself so *Us Weekly* will stop saying I should be dating James Franco instead. Which is stupid, but what can I do about it?'

'James Franco!' Lilly burst out. 'Well. Whatever. James Franco *is* pretty cute.'

'Not as cute as Michael,' I said.

'Ew,' Lilly said, but only because she routinely says *ew* to any reference to her brother being cute.

Then, since she was feeling so bad for me and all, I figured I might as well take advantage of the situation. So I went, 'Did you and J.P. sleep together this summer, or what?'

But Lilly just laughed.

'Nice try, POG,' she said. 'But I don't feel THAT sorry for you.'

Dang.

Wednesday, September 8, Intro to Creative Writing

Describe a scene outside your window:

The young girl sits on the swing, her heart heavy, her eyes swollen with tears. The world as she's known it has ceased to exist. She will never again know what it is to laugh with childish abandon, because her childhood is behind her. Crushed hopes and disappointed dreams will be her constant companions now that the love of her life has flown. She raises her eyes to watch a plane as it soars across the brilliantly lit sky, the sun sinking in the west. Is that the plane carrying away her love? Probably. It disappears into the crimson sunset.

F-

Mia, when I said describe a scene outside your window, I meant for you to describe something you actually see outside your window, such as a dumpster or bodega. I did not want you to make up some scene. And I know you made up the scene above, because there is no way you could have known what the girl on the swing (if you can even see swings from your window, which I doubt, since I happen to know you live in NoHo and there are no swings there that I am aware of) was thinking unless that girl happened to be you, in which case you could not have seen her, because you cannot see yourself, except in mirrors. Please redo this, actually following the assignment this time. I make these assignments for a reason and I expect you to complete them AS WRITTEN.

L. Martinez

Wednesday, September 8, English

Mia!!! I heard. Are you all right????

Honestly, T. I just don't know.

But you realize it's a GOOD thing. I mean, for Michael.

I know.

And you can always go visit him! I mean, you have your own jet!!!

Oh, right. That'll happen.

Wait - Are you being sarcastic?

Yes, I'm being sarcastic. My dad is never going to let me to go to Japan, Tina. Not to see Michael.

Well, then get him to let you go to visit the Princess of Japan - you're friends with her, right? I mean, you really like her kid. And then while you're there, you can see Michael.

Thanks, Tina. It doesn't actually work that way, but it doesn't matter anyway. Because whenever I get time off from school, I have to go to Genovia. Remember? Besides, the truth is, even if I went to Japan, I'm not so sure Michael would want to see me.

What? Of course he would! What are you talking about?

He's not JUST going for his robotic arm thingy. He's also going to get away from me.

What? That's crazy! What makes you think THAT?

Because he SAID so. He said it's really hard to be around me so much and not . . . you know.

Oh. My. God. That is the most romantic thing I have ever heard in my life!!!!!!!!!!!

TINA!!! It is not romantic!!!!

He LOOOOOOVES you! You should be GLAD!!!

Glad that my boyfriend is moving to another country because he's tired of taking so many cold showers? Yeah. Right.

You're being sarcastic again, aren't you?

Yes.

Mia, don't you see? The whole thing is SOOOO romantic: Michael is just like Aragorn from *The Lord of the Rings*. Remember when Aragorn was all in love with Arwen, but he didn't feel worthy of her, because she was an elfin princess, and her dad wouldn't let him marry her until he'd reclaimed his throne and proved he was more than just some mortal guy?

Um. Yeah.

MICHAEL IS RECLAIMING HIS THRONE SO HE CAN PROVE HE IS WORTHY OF YOU!!!!! JUST LIKE ARAGORN. And, OK, he's doing it by inventing some thing none of us understands except him. But that doesn't matter. He's DOING IT FOR YOU.

And the thousands of people whose lives might be saved by it. And the millions of dollars he could potentially make if it works.

But don't you see? All of that is part of what he's doing FOR YOU.

But I don't *care* about any of that stuff, Tina. I mean, I want him to be happy and all. But I would be happier if he'd just stay here so I could smell his neck every day!!!!

Well, you might have to sacrifice neck-smellage for a while in order for Michael to find self-actualization. I mean, in the long run, what he's doing now will guarantee you constant neck-smellage in the future. Because if he becomes a millionaire or whatever, there's NO WAY your grandma or anyone else can stand in the way of the two of you being together, because you could just run off with him, even if you get cut off from your Genovian fortune or your dad makes you abdicate the throne, or whatever. See?

I guess. I just don't see why he can't achieve self-actualization here in AMERICA.

I don't know either. But I do know that Michael loves you, and that's all that matters!!!!!!!

Everything is so simple in Tinaland. I so wish I lived there instead of here, in the cruel, cold Real World.

Wednesday, September 8, French

The thing is, deep down I know Tina is right.

But I just can't get as enthusiastic about it as she is. Maybe because Aragorn, even though he was faithful to Arwen while he was off finding himself and all, still had that thing going on with Eowyn. Whatever that was.

What's to keep Michael from having the same kind of thing with some brilliant Japanese geisha/robotics engineer?

La speakerine de la chaîne douze a dit, 'Maintenant, croyantes, un petit film – le premier film d'une série de six. Mesdames, voici le film que vous avez attendu pendant des semaines. Un film remarquable, un film qui a changé ma vie et la vie d'autres femmes dans le monde. Oui, Le Mérite Incroyable d'une Femme.'

$61 + 55 = 116$

I passed Lana in the hallway on the way to class, and she went, 'Hey, Pete! How's Neverland?' which made her new clone as well as her evil henchwoman Trish laugh so hard that Diet Coke came out of their noses.

I don't know for sure, because I've never been able to get all the way through *The Lord of the Rings* due to that fact that there are hardly any parts with girl characters in it (so I have to pretend Merry is a girl hobbit). But I'm fairly certain this never happened to Arwen.

Wednesday, September 8, Lunch

So I was sitting here, innocently eating my falafel with tahini, when Ling Su sat down across from me and went, 'Mia. How *are* you?' with her eyes all big and sympathetic.

I went, 'Um. Fine.'

Then Perin sat down next to me and was like, 'Mia. We *heard*. Are you OK?'

God. News travels fast around this school.

'I'm fine,' I said, trying to smile bravely. Which is no joke when you've got a big wad of falafel in your mouth.

'I can't believe it,' Shameeka said. She doesn't even normally EAT at our table, since she's usually too busy spying for us over at the jock/cheerleader table. But all of a sudden, she'd put her tray down next to Perin's. 'Is he really moving to *JAPAN*?'

'Looks like it,' I said. It's funny, but every time I hear the word Japan now, my heart does this funny twisty thing. The way it used to do when I heard the word Buffy, back when the TV show *Buffy the Vampire Slayer* was ending.

'You should dump him,' Boris said after joining us.

'BORIS!' Tina looked shocked. 'Mia, ignore him. He doesn't know what he's talking about.'

'Yes I do,' Boris said. 'I know exactly what I'm talking about. This happens in orchestras all the time. Two musicians fall in love, then one gets a better paying job at another rival orchestra in another city, or even another country. They always try to make it work – the long-distance thing – but it never does. Sooner or later one of them always falls in love with a clarinettist, and that's it. Long-distance relationships never work. You

65

should dump him now, so it's a nice clean break, and move on. End of story.'

Tina was staring at her boyfriend in shock. 'Boris! That's the most horrible thing to say! How could you *say* that?'

Boris didn't get it, though. He just shrugged and went, 'What? It's the truth. Everyone knows it.'

'My brother isn't going to fall in love with someone else,' Lilly said, in a bored voice, from where she sat down the table, across from J.P. 'OK? He's completely besotted with Mia.'

'Ha,' Tina said, giving Boris a poke with her straw. 'See?'

'I am only telling it the way I've experienced it,' Boris said. 'Maybe Michael won't fall in love with a clarinettist. But Mia will.'

'BORIS!' Tina looked outraged. 'What on EARTH would make you say that???'

'Yeah, Boris,' Lilly said, looking at him like he was a bug she'd found in her hummus. 'What's this thing you've apparently got for clarinettists? I thought you considered woodwinds to be beneath you.'

'I am merely stating a fact,' Boris said, putting down his fork with a bang to illustrate his seriousness. 'Mia is only sixteen years old. And they aren't married. Michael shouldn't think that he can just go off to a foreign country and that she is going to wait for him. It isn't fair to her. She should be allowed to move on with her life, date other people and have fun, not sit in her room every Saturday night for a year until he gets back.'

I saw Shameeka and Ling Su exchange glances. Ling Su even made an '*Oops, he might actually be right*' face.

Tina didn't think he was right though.

'Are you saying that if you got a job as first violin with the London Philharmonic you wouldn't want me to wait for you?' she asked her boyfriend.

'Of course I would *want* you to wait,' Boris explained. 'But I wouldn't ASK you to. It wouldn't be fair. But I know you WOULD wait, anyway, because that's the kind of girl you are.'

'Mia's that kind of girl too!' Tina said decidedly.

'No,' Boris said, gravely shaking his head. 'I don't think so.'

'That's OK, Boris,' I said quickly, before Tina's head exploded. 'I WANT to sit in my room every Saturday night until Michael gets back.'

Boris looked at me like I was nuts. 'You DO?'

'Yes,' I said. 'I do. Because I love Michael and if I can't be with him, I'd rather not be with any boy.'

Boris just shook his head sadly.

'That's what all the couples in my orchestra say,' he said. 'And eventually, one of them gets tired of sitting in their room. Next thing you know, they've hooked up with a clarinettist. There's *always* a clarinettist.'

This was very disconcerting. I was sitting there, feeling the same panic rising I feel every time I think of Michael's leaving – just three more days! Three more days until he's gone – when I happened to notice that J.P. was looking at me.

And then when I met his gaze, he smiled at me. And rolled his eyes. As if to say, *'Listen to the crazy Russian violinist! Isn't he silly?'*

And suddenly, the panic disappeared and I felt all right again.

I smiled back and, reaching for my falafel, said, 'I think Michael and I will be OK, Boris.'

'Of *course* you will,' Tina said. And then Boris yelped. It was clear Tina had kicked him from beneath the table.

I hope she left a bruise.

Wednesday, September 8, Gifted and Talented

So Lilly didn't even give me twenty-four hours to recover from the blow her brother delivered. No, she started harping on about the student government campaign again during G and T.

'Listen, POG,' she said. 'I know you were the only person nominated for student-council president, but you can't win if at least fifty per cent of the class doesn't vote for you.'

'Who else are they going to vote for?' I wanted to know. 'Especially if no one else is running?'

'Write-ins,' Lilly said. 'Themselves. Who knows? You could end up being beaten by Lana anyway, even though she's technically not running. You know her little sister just entered ninth grade, right?'

This information was meaningless to me. I mean, on account of my head being completely full of the fact that MY BOYFRIEND IS MOVING TO JAPAN FOR A YEAR (or more).

'Did you hear me, Mia?' Lilly was peering at me all concernedly over her student-government binder. 'Gretchen Weinberger is exactly like her older sis . . . only with a bigger chip on her shoulder. Think of that documentary we saw on MTV *True Life* on 'roid rage, and you'll have a clear picture. Gretchen could undoubtedly rally the entire ninth grade against you if she wanted to. And, if you've had any kind of look at them, you can clearly see this freshman class is the most apathetic bunch of bottom feeders that have ever walked the planet . . . I actually heard one of them insisting that global warming is all a myth because Michael Crichton said so in that most recent pathetic excuse for a book of his.'

I just looked at her some more. Was Gretchen Weinberger the clone – that slightly smaller version of Lana I'd seen laughing in the hallway over the elder Weinberger's witticism concerning my haircut and Neverland? Probably. I'd just assumed at the time she was another Lana wannabe. It makes sense she's her sister.

'But that idiot's remarks about that anti-science schlockmeister Crichton gave me an idea,' Lilly went on. 'This is a generation that's pretty much been raised on fear – fear of feminists, who as we all know are out to destroy family values (ha, ha), fear of terrorists, fear of getting a bad SAT score and then not getting into Yale or Princeton and therefore being a failure and having to go to some less-well-known school from which they might – gasp – have to get an entry-level job after graduation, making one hundred thousand dollars a year instead of one hundred and five thousand dollars a year. I say we play on these fears and use them to our advantage.'

'How are we going to do that?' I asked. Not that I cared. 'And also, technically, we're the same generation as Lana's little sister. I mean, we're older than she is. But she's still our generation.'

'No, she isn't,' Lilly said, with a gleam in her eye – a gleam I did not trust for one second. 'She was born just late enough not to have been cognitively aware of *Party of Five*, and that makes us generationally separate. And I think I know EXACTLY where their weak spot is. I'm working on it. I should have everything ready by tomorrow. Don't worry, POG. They'll be BEGGING you to be their student-body president by the time I'm done with them.'

'Wow,' I said. 'Well, thanks. But, see, the thing is, Lilly . . . I don't think I want to run for student-body president this year.'

Lilly just blinked at me. 'What?'

I took a deep breath. This wasn't going to be easy.

'It's just . . . well, you know what I got in math on my practice PSAT. And I have Pre-Calculus AND Chemistry this year. I swear to God it's only been one day, and I don't have the slightest idea what anybody is talking about in either of those courses. I mean, not even A LITTLE. I really think I need to concentrate on school work this year. I just don't think I'm going to have time to run the school too. Not with all that and princess stuff.'

Lilly raised one eyebrow. I hate it when she does this. Because she knows how and I don't.

'This is because of my brother, isn't it,' she said. It wasn't a question.

'Of course not,' I said.

'Because,' Lilly said, 'I mean, if anything, now that he's leaving, you're going to have MORE time on your hands. Not less.'

'Yes,' I said, with some asperity. 'But also, now that he's leaving, I'm not going to have anybody to help me with me Pre-Calc and Chem homework. I'm going to have get a tutor or something. And tutors, unlike Michael, aren't totally willing to come over and help me with a worksheet at ten o'clock on a Wednesday night after I've been at a student-council meeting and then some state dinner over at the Genovian Embassy.'

Lilly didn't look very sympathetic. 'I can't believe

71

you're doing this to me,' she said. 'You're more apathetic than the rest of this school. You're worse than the ninth-graders!'

'Lilly,' I said. 'I totally think you could win, without my help. I mean, for one thing, think about it – you'd be running unopposed.'

'You know I wouldn't get fifty per cent of the vote,' Lilly said through gritted teeth. 'Why can't you just run and step down, like you were SUPPOSED to do last year?'

'Because my boyfriend is leaving this country for a whole year in THREE DAYS,' I practically yelled, causing Mrs Hill to glance up from her Isabella Bird catalogue. I lowered my voice. 'And I want to spend as much time as I can with him until then. Which means I DON'T want to be spending my evenings writing speeches and making *Mia For President* signs.'

'I'll write the speeches,' Lilly said, her teeth still gritted. 'And I'll make the signs. You just do what you were supposed to last year, and step down like you said you were going to.'

'Oh God, *whatever*,' I said, just to get her off my back. 'FINE.'

'FINE,' Lilly said back.

And then it occurred to me that I was letting a golden opportunity slip through my fingers, and I added, 'ON ONE CONDITION.'

And Lilly was like, 'What?'

'You have to tell me if you and J.P. Did It over the summer.'

Lilly just glared at me for a while. Then, finally, like it was this supreme sacrifice, she said, 'All right. I'll tell you. AFTER the election.'

Which was fine with me. So long as I get to find out.

I don't know why it's so interesting to me. But, I mean, if my best friend has had sex, I think I should be allowed to hear about it. In detail. Especially considering the fact that I'm not going to be able even to SMELL my boyfriend for the coming year, and will have to live vicariously through Lilly's romance.

Although she once told me she doesn't go around smelling J.P.'s neck and thinks it's very weird that I smell Michael's all the time.

More than likely Lilly's vomeronasal organ – her auxiliary olfactory sense organ – regressed during gestation like most humans' do. Mine obviously didn't.

Which is just another example of what a biological sport I am.

Mrs Hill just asked me what I plan on doing in class this year. So I was forced to tell her about my practice PSAT math score.

Now she's got me doing practice problems from the *Official SAT Study Guide*.

I think that this, coupled with the rest of the events in the past twenty-four hours of my life, pretty much proves that God does not exist.

Or that if He does, He is supremely indifferent to my suffering.

Jill bought five apples at the grocery store. She paid with a five-dollar bill and received three quarters in change. Jill realized she'd received too much change, and gave back one of the quarters. How much did the apples cost?

WHATEVER. That is what debit cards are for. OK, let's move on.

What is the smallest positive integer divisible by the numbers two, three, four, and five?

Oh, right. Like I know. OK, next.

The weight of the cookies in a box of a hundred cookies is eight ounces. What is the weight, in ounces, of three cookies?

WHY DO I NEED TO KNOW THIS IF ALL I'M GOING TO BE DOING SOMEDAY IS RUNNING A COUNTRY AND WILL HAVE MY OWN ROYAL ACCOUNTANTS? WHY, WHY, WHY???? IT ISN'T FAIR!!!!!!!!!!

Wednesday, September 8, Chemistry

Mia – Is it true? Michael is going to Tsukuba for a year to work on a robotic device that could put an end to open-heart surgery?

Oh God. Here we go. Tina insists Kenny is still in love with me – even after all this time – but I've always told her she is confusing her Harlequin romance novels with real life again.

But maybe I was being unnecessarily harsh. Maybe she's RIGHT. Because why else would he be so interested in my current dating status????

Yes, Kenny. It's true. Although we are not breaking up!!!

That is SO COOL. Do you think he'd consider hiring me – you know, when he gets back – as like an intern or something? Because I've always been fascinated by robotics, and have actually been tinkering with a design for an orbital rotor for a robotic scalpel. Do you think he could use me? I assume he'll be hiring his friends . . .

Oh. So, it's not me he wants after all . . . well, that's a relief.

Kenny, you KNOW about this robotic surgery stuff?

Um, of course. And it isn't 'stuff', Mia, it's really the new frontier in robotic science. Robotic surgical systems are already being installed in hospitals around the globe. The ultimate goal of the robotic field is to design a system that will do exactly what Michael's prototype does. If he can build a model that actually operates as it's supposed to in a surgical setting . . . well, let's just say there won't have been as ground-shaking a development in science since Lucy the cloned sheep. Michael will be hailed as a genius . . . no, more than just a genius. Perhaps even a MEDICAL SAVIOUR.

Oh. Well. Thanks for clarifying that for me. I'll be sure to put in a good word for you to Michael.

Sweet. Thanks! ☺

Mia – you OK? You hardly touched your falafel at lunch.

God, J.P. is so sweet! I can't believe he noticed!

I'm fine. I guess.

I don't imagine Boris pontificating on orchestral dalliances he has seen helped very much.

Yeah, not so much. It's just . . . what's a medical saviour going to want to have to do with ME? I mean, I'm just a PRINCESS. Anybody can be a *princess*. All you have to do is have the right parents. It's no harder than being born Paris Hilton, for God's sake.

At least you remember to put on underwear in the morning, I'm assuming.

Is that supposed to be helping?

Sorry. I thought the situation called for a little levity. Bad miscalculation on my part. Mia, you're wonderful in and of yourself. You know that. You're a lot more than just a princess. In fact, I would say that's the tiniest part of you, not what DEFINES you.

But I haven't DONE anything. I mean, not anything great that people are going to remember me by. Except be a princess, which, as I mentioned, isn't something I actively DID, I just got born that way.

You're only sixteen. Cut yourself some slack.

But Michael's only nineteen and he may be saving thousands of people's lives, like, next year. If I'm going to do something great someday, I need to get started NOW.

I thought you were going to write a screenplay of your life and Lilly was going to direct it.

Yeah, but what have I done in my LIFE that will make the screenplay meaningful? Like, I haven't saved hundreds of Jews from annihilation by the Nazi scourge, or gone blind and yet gone on to write beautiful music.

I think holding yourself to the standards set by Oskar Schindler and Stevie Wonder is a bit unrealistic.

But don't you see? MICHAEL is setting that kind of standard.

> But Michael loves you, just the way you are! So what are you worried about? You can be a great person just for being a good friend or a terrific writer or humorous to be around, you know.

I guess. It's just that he's probably going to be meeting a lot of brilliant, beautiful girls in Japan, and how do I know he's not going to fall for one of THEM?

> He's probably met lots of brilliant, beautiful girls at Columbia, and he hasn't fallen for any of them, has he?

Well, no. But that's just because, even though they're all brilliant, they all look like Judith Gershner.

> Who's Judith Gershner?

She's this girl who used to go here who could clone fruit flies and who I thought Michael liked and – you know what? Never mind. You're right. I'm being ridiculous.

> I didn't say you were being ridiculous. I said you were being too hard on yourself. You're a great person, and if in the unlikely event Michael were ever to imply otherwise, I will happily kick his ass for you.

Ha. Thanks. But that's what I have Lars for.

Mia — not to be a jerk, but if you want to pass this class, you'd better stop passing notes with J.P. and pay attention. I know I'm your lab partner, but I'm not taking up the slack if you start to fall behind.

OK, Kenny. Sorry. You're right.

BUSTED!!!!

Shut up, you're making me laugh!!!!!!!!!
I'm paying attention now.

The Archimedes Principle: volume of a solid is equal to the volume of water it displaces.

Densities of typical solids and liquids in g/ml

Substance	Density
Gasoline	0.68
Ice	0.92
Water	1.00
Salt	2.16
Iron	7.86
Lead	11.38
Mercury	13.55
Gold	19.30

I realize Chemistry is important, you know, in our daily lives and everything. But seriously. What possible use is knowing the density of gasoline going to be in my future capacity as ruler of Genovia?

Wednesday, September 8, Pre-Calc

Composite function = combination of two functions
  f (g (x)) does NOT = g (f (x))
A relation is any collection of points on the xy coordinate system

Constant function = horizontal line
Horizontal line has 0 slope

Oh.
My.
God.
This.
Is.
So.
Boring.

Homework

Homeroom: N/A
Intro to Creative Writing: Describe a person that you know
English: *Franny and Zooey*
French: Continue *décrire un soir amusant avec les amis*
G and T: N/A
PE: N/A
Chemistry: Whatever, Kenny will tell me
Pre-Calculus: ??????

Wednesday, September 8, the Limo on the way home from the Ritz Carlton

When I walked into Grandmere's suite at the Ritz today (the W was apparently so unsatisfactory, she only stayed one night), I was totally shocked to find my father there.

I'd forgotten he was coming into town for the UN's General Assembly.

And *he*'d apparently forgotten that it's never a good idea to drop by to see Grandmere before cocktail hour (she's been told by her physician that she can't have any more three-Sidecar luncheons if she doesn't want her angina acting up) because she is more than a little cranky.

'Look at this!' she was saying as she shook a pillow in my dad's face. 'Mere seven-hundred-thread-count sheets! It's scandalous! No wonder Rommel has a rash!'

'Rommel always has a rash,' my dad said tiredly. Then he noticed I'd come in, and he said, 'Hi, honey. Long time no – *what happened to your hair?*'

I didn't even bother getting offended. Having your boyfriend announce he's moving to Japan has a way of causing you to get your priorities straight.

'I got it cut,' I said. 'I don't care if you don't like it. I don't have to mess with it any more and that's all that matters. To me, anyway.'

'Oh,' Dad said. 'It's, uh. Cute. What's the matter?'

'What? Nothing.'

'Something's the matter, Mia. I can tell.'

'It's really nothing,' I assured him. Just the knowledge that all my parents have to do is look at my face and know something is wrong made me realize how very much I must actually be hurting from this Michael thing. Because I'm TRYING to hide it. I really am. For Michael's sake. Because I know I should be excited and happy for him.

And I AM excited and happy for him.

Except for the part where I'm weeping. On the inside.

'Are you listening to me, Philippe?' Grandmere was demanding. 'You know Rommel requires eight-hundred-thread-count sheets *at the very least*.'

Dad sighed. 'I'll have some thousand-count sheets sent over from Bergdorfs, all right? Mia, I know something's wrong. What's your mother done now? Got arrested at another one of her war protests? I've *told* her to stop chaining herself to things.'

'It's not *Mom*,' I said, throwing myself on to a brocade-covered chaise longue. 'She hasn't chained herself to anything in *years*.'

'Well, she's a very . . . unpredictable woman,' my dad said. Which is his way of saying, as nicely as possible, that Mom is flighty and irresponsible about a lot of things. But not her kids. 'But you're right, I shouldn't jump to conclusions. It's nothing to do with Frank, is it? The two of them are getting along all right? It's very stressful having a new baby in the house. Or so I hear.'

I rolled my eyes. My dad always wants the scoop on what's going on with Mom and Mr Gianini. Which is sort of hilarious, because there's never actually anything going on with them. Unless you mean their fights over what to watch at breakfast, CNN (Mr G) or MTV (Mom). Mom can't stand politics first thing in the morning. She prefers Panic! At The Disco.

'It isn't just the sheets, Philippe,' Grandmere was

going on. 'Do you realize the televisions in the rooms of this hotel are only *twenty-seven inches* wide?'

'You say there's nothing on American television but filth and violence,' my dad said, staring at his mother in astonishment.

'Well, yes,' Grandmere said. 'There isn't. Except for *Judge Judy.*'

'It's just . . . *everything*,' I said, ignoring Grandmere. Because Dad was now ignoring her too. 'It's only two days into the semester, and it's already my worst one ever. Ms Martinez stuck me in Intro to Creative Writing. Intro stands for INTRODUCTION. I don't need to be introduced to creative writing. I eat, sleep and breathe creative writing. And don't even get me started on Chemistry and Pre-Calculus. But the worst is . . . well, it's Michael.'

Dad didn't look surprised to hear this. In fact, he looked pleased.

'Well now, Mia, I hate to tell you this but . . . I suspected this might be coming. Michael's in college now, and you're still in high school, and you have to spend a lot of time on your royal duties and in Genovia, and you can't expect a young man in his prime to simply wait around for you. It's natural that Michael might find a young lady closer to his own age who actually has the time to spend doing the kinds of things college-age kids do – things that are simply not appropriate for a high-school-aged princess to take part in.'

'Dad.' I blinked at him. 'Michael didn't break up with me. At least if that's what you meant by that speech you just gave me.'

'He didn't?' Dad stopped looking so pleased. 'Oh. Well, what *did* he do then?'

'He – well, remember when you flew back to Genovia with me and we watched *The Lord of the Rings* during the flight?'

'Yes.' Dad raised his eyebrows. 'Are you telling me Michael's come into possession of the One Ring?'

'No,' I said. I couldn't believe he was trying to make a joke out of it. 'But he's trying to prove himself to the elf king, like Aragorn.'

'Who's the elf king?' Dad asked, like he genuinely didn't know.

'Dad. YOU'RE the elf king.'

'Really?' Dad adjusted his tie, looking pleased again. Then he stopped. 'Wait . . . my ears aren't pointy. Are they?'

'I meant FIGURATIVELY, Dad,' I said, rolling my eyes. 'Michael feels like he has to prove himself in order to be with your daughter. Just like Aragorn felt he had to prove himself to win the elf king's approval to be with Arwen.'

'Well,' Dad said. 'I don't see what's wrong with that. Only how exactly does he plan on doing it? Winning my approval, I mean? Because, I'm sorry, but leading an army of the dead to defeat the Orcs isn't really going to cut the mustard with me.'

'Michael isn't leading an army of the dead anywhere. He's inventing a robotic surgical arm that will allow surgeons to do heart surgery without opening up the chest,' I said.

That wiped the smirk clean off Dad's face.

'Really?' he asked in a totally different tone. 'Michael did that?'

'Well, he has a prototype for it,' I explained. 'And some Japanese company is flying him out there so he can help them to build a working model. Or something. The thing is, it's going to take a YEAR! Michael is going to be in Tsukuba for a YEAR! Or more!'

'A year,' Dad repeated. 'Or more. Well. That's a very long time.'

'Yes, it's a very long time,' I said dramatically. 'And while he's thousands of miles away, inventing cool stuff, I'm going to be stuck in stupid Intro to Creative Writing and eleventh-grade Chem, which I'm already flunking, not to mention Pre-Calc, which, once again, I don't even know why I have to learn, since we've got all those accountants—'

'Now, now,' Dad said. 'Everyone has to learn calculus in order to be a well-rounded individual.'

'You know what would make me a well-rounded individual, and you a celebrated philanthropist and possibly even named *Time* magazine's Person of the Year?' I asked. 'Well, I'll tell you: If you founded your own robotics lab right here in New York City that Michael could build his robotic-arm thingy in!'

My dad got a good laugh out of that one.

Which was nice. Except that I wasn't joking.

'I'm serious, Dad,' I said. 'I mean, why not? It's not like you don't have the money.'

'Mia,' my dad said, sobering. 'I don't know anything about robotics labs.'

'But Michael does,' I said. 'He could tell you what he'd need. And then you could just, you know. Pay for it. And you'd totally get credit when Michael successfully completes his robotic-arm thingy. They'd put you on *Larry King*, I'll bet. Who cares about *Vogue* . . . think of how much Genovia would be in the press *then*. It would do WONDERS for tourism. Which you must admit has been on the wane since the dollar tanked.'

'Mia,' Dad said, shaking his head. 'It's out of the question. I'm very pleased for Michael – I always thought he had potential. But I am not going to spend millions of dollars building some robotics laboratory so you can fritter away eleventh grade necking with your boyfriend instead of passing Pre-Calculus.'

I glared at him. 'Nobody calls it necking any more, Dad.'

Well, I had to say SOMETHING. Also . . . *fritter*?

'Excuse me.' Grandmere stomped over until she stood in the middle of the room and could glare at both of us at the same time. 'I'm so sorry to interrupt your very important discussion of THAT BOY. But I'm wondering if the two of you have noticed something about this room. Something that is very obviously MISSING.'

Dad and I looked around. Grandmere's 1,530-square-foot penthouse suite came complete with two bedrooms; two and a half bathrooms – each of which contained a marble soaking tub with separate stall shower, a twelve-inch flat-screen television, exclusive Frédéric Fekkai and Cote Bastide bath amenities, Floris shaving kit and Frette candles; a living room; a dining room with seating for eight; a separate pantry; a library of books, DVD player, stereo, selection of DVDs and in-room compact-disc selection, multi-line cordless telephone with voice-mail and data line capabilities, high-speed internet access and a floor model telescope so she could look out at the stars or across the park into Woody Allen's apartment.

There was nothing Grandmere's suite didn't have. NOTHING.

'AN ASHTRAY!' Grandmere shouted. 'THIS IS A NON-SMOKING SUITE!!!'

Dad looked up at the ceiling. Then he sighed. Then he said, 'Mia. If Michael, as you say, is intent on proving himself worthy of you to me, then he wouldn't want my help anyway. I'm sorry you're going to have be separated from him for a year, but I think buckling down and concentrating exclusively on your studies might not be such a bad thing. Mother.' He looked at Grandmere. 'You are impossible. But I will get you a suite at another hotel. Let me make a few phone calls,' and walked into the dining room to do so.

Grandmere, looking very self-satisfied, opened her purse, plucked out the key card to her suite, and placed it on the coffee table in front of me.

'Well,' she said. 'What a shame. Looks like I'll be moving. Again.'

'Grandmere,' I said. She was making me SO MAD. 'Did you know there are people who are still living in TENTS and FEMA TRAILERS because of all the hurricanes and tsunamis and earthquakes there've been in various parts of the world? And you're complaining that you can't SMOKE in your room? There is nothing wrong with this suite. It's totally beautiful. It's every bit as nice as your suite back at the Plaza. You're just being ridiculous, because you don't like change.'

'I suppose that's true,' Grandmere said with a sigh, as she sat down in one of the brocade-covered armchairs across from the couch I was sitting on. 'But I believe my folly might be to your advantage.'

'Oh?' I was barely listening to her. I couldn't believe how quickly my dad had shot down my Build-Your-Own-Lab idea. I really thought it had been a good one. I mean, I know I only came up with it on the spur of the moment. But it seemed like something he might go for. He's always building hospital wings over in Genovia, and then naming them after himself. I think the Prince Philippe Renaldo Surgical Robotic Systems Lab has a nice ring to it.

'The suite is paid for through the rest of the week,' Grandmere said, leaning over to tap on the key card she'd left on the table. 'I won't be staying here of course. But there's no reason why you shouldn't feel free to use it, if you like.'

'What am I going to do with a suite at the Ritz, Grandmere?' I demanded. 'It might have escaped your notice, because you're so preoccupied with your own quote suffering unquote. But I am hardly going to be hosting any slumber parties this week. I am in a full-on life crisis.'

Grandmere's gaze hardened on me. 'Sometimes,' she said, 'I cannot believe that you and I are related by blood.'

'Welcome to my world,' I said.

'Well, the rooms are yours,' Grandmere said, sliding the key card closer to me. 'To do with whatever it is you wish. Personally, if I still lived with my parents, and my paramour was leaving on a year-long quest to prove himself to MY father, I'd use the rooms to stage a very private and very romantic goodbye. But that's just me. I've always been a very passionate woman, very in touch with my emotions. I've often noticed that I—'

Blah, blah, blah. Grandmere's voice went on and on. And on. Dad came back into the room and told her he'd got her a suite at the Four Seasons, so then she rang for her maid and made her start packing for the third time this week alone.

And that was my princess lesson for the day.

Good thing I'm not paying for these, because the quality has really started going downhill.

I think I'm hallucinating from being dehydrated, or something. I have all the symptoms:

- Extreme thirst.
- Dry mouth with no saliva.
- Dry eyes; no tears.
- Decreased urination, or urinating three or fewer times in twenty-four hours.
- Arms and legs that may feel cool to the touch.
- Feeling very tired, restless, or irritable.
- Lightheadedness that is relieved by lying down.

Of course, I generally experience all these symptoms after spending any amount of time with Grandmere.

Still, I'm drinking all the bottled water in the limo, just to be on the safe side.

Wednesday, September 8, the Loft

Michael wants to do a whole bunch of New Yorky things before he leaves on Friday. Tonight we're eating at his favourite burger place, Corner Bistro, in the West Village. He swears they're the best hamburgers in the city – outside Johnny Rockets.

Except that Michael won't go to Johnny Rockets because he doesn't believe in food chains – he says they are contributing to the homogenization of America, and that as chain stores force out locally owned restaurants and businesses, communities will lose everything that once made them unique, and America will become just one big strip mall, with every single community consisting of nothing but Wal-Marts, McDonald's, a Jiffylube and an Applebee's, and instead of being a melting pot, America will be mayonnaise.

Still, I happen to know Michael's not above sneaking out for a St Louis and a black-and-white from time to time.

Of course, being a vegetarian I can't actually join him in his quest for One Last Perfect Burger before leaving for the Far East. I'll just have a salad. And some fries. Mom is cool with me going out on a school night because she knows it's Michael's last week being in the same hemisphere as me. Mr G tried to say something about my Pre-Calc homework – I guess he and Ms Hong must talk in the Teachers' Lounge or whatever – but Mom just gave him A Look, and he shut up. I'm lucky I have such cool parents.

Well, except for Dad. I can't believe he said no to my brilliant Build-Your-Own-Lab idea. It's his loss, I guess. I'm not going to tell Michael about it. I mean, that I actually asked. I'm not sure, even if my dad HAD agreed to build his own robotics lab, that Michael would have wanted to work there, on account of the whole Wanting-To-Get-Away-From-Me-On-Account-Of-The-No-Sex thing.

And I'm DEFINITELY not telling him about the hotel key Grandmere gave me. If Michael found out I had a hotel suite all to myself, he'd totally want to—

OH.

MY.

GOD.

Wednesday, September 8, Corner Bistro

I have to write fast. Michael just went up to the counter for more napkins. I don't know where our waitress disappeared to. This place is a zoo. Someone must have spilt the beans about the burgers in some guidebook. A Big Apple double-decker tour bus just pulled up and puked about a hundred tourists into the restaurant.

Anyway, right as Michael arrived to pick me up, it hit me. What Grandmere was REALLY doing, giving me that key: *Use the rooms to stage a very private and very romantic goodbye.* Grandmere HAD to be implying what I think she was implying.

Grandmere has given me her suite at the Ritz for

SEX!!!!

Seriously! Grandmere's giving me her suite at the Ritz so I can use it to 'say goodbye' to Michael. In the kind of privacy we could never find anywhere else, what with neither of us having our own place.

In other words, my grandmother has given me her own version of the Precious Gift: THE most precious gift any teenager could ask for:

MY GRANDMOTHER HAS GIVEN ME MY OWN SEX PLACE!!!!!

I know it seems unbelievable. But it's true. There's no other explanation for it. Grandmere wants me to have sex with my boyfriend the night before he leaves for Japan.

Only why would my own grandmother be *encouraging* me to give away my Precious Gift when I am still just a teen? Grandmothers are supposed to be old-fashioned and want their grandchildren to wait until marriage before consummating their relationships. Grandmothers don't believe in trying the pants on before you buy them. Grandmothers all say the same thing: 'He isn't going to buy the cow if he can get the milk for free.' Grandmothers are supposed to want what's best for their offspring's offspring.

Could Grandmere really think having goodbye sex with my boyfriend in her abandoned suite at the Ritz is what's BEST for me?

Unless . . .

OH MY GOD. This just hit me: What if Grandmere is trying to help me keep Michael from going to Japan????

Seriously. Because what guy, given the choice between sex and no sex, would choose no sex? I mean, Michael is basically moving to Japan because of the whole no-sex thing.

Well, aside from the whole saving-thousands-of-lives-and-making-millions-and-proving-his-worth-to-my-family-and-*Us-Weekly* thing.

But if he knew he had a chance at sex, wouldn't he . . . stay?

I know. It's CRAZY.

So crazy, in fact, it just might work.

No. NO!!!! I can't believe I wrote that!!!! It's wrong!!!! I mean, to use sex as a means to manipulate someone. It goes against my feminist principles. God, what could Grandmere be THINKING?

Except of course Grandmere doesn't HAVE any

feminist principles. Well, I mean, she does, she just doesn't think of them that way.

And then of course there's the whole Waiting-Until-Prom-Night thing. I mean, I promised Tina. We PROMISED each other we'd hold on to our Precious Gifts until prom night.

But that was before. Before Michael decided he had to go on this crazy robot-arm quest.

Surely Tina would understand –

Wait. Am I really considering this? No! No, it's wrong! It's horrible! I could never do something like that! I would be robbing the world of Michael's robotic arm thingy! I can't do something like that. I'm a *PRINCESS*, for crying out loud.

But what if – just what if – Michael and I had sex in Grandmere's abandoned suite at the Ritz and he liked it so much he decided not to go after all? Wouldn't that be WORTH compromising my feminist principles? Wouldn't it, actually, be MORE feminist, because by keeping Michael around I will be able to smell his neck and therefore release serotonin into my brain on a regular basis, making me a calmer and more well-rounded individual, and a better student leader and role model to young girls everywhere?

AHHHHHH, Michael's back with the napkins. More later.

Wednesday, September 8, 11 p.m., the Loft

Well. That was very nice. We had a lovely dinner, followed by cupcakes from Magnolia Bakery (yes, the one from 'Lazy Sunday' on *Saturday Night Live*).

Then we made out all emotionally for half an hour in the vestibule of my apartment building while Lars pretended to be putting money in the parking meter, even though the limo has diplomatic plates and we never get ticketed.

I really don't think it's the extremely high levels of serotonin batting around in my brain right now due to smelling Michael's neck for so long (not to mention oxytocin, a hormone that rushes to the brain in moments of intense sexual pleasure, and which is why in Health and Safety they advised us not to have sex with anyone we hadn't known for a while, due to the fact that oxytocin can cloud your judgment and make you feel like you're in love with someone when in fact it's really just the oxytocin, and you really have nothing in common at all, or even actually like one another. Which basically explains why Grandpere married Grandmere).

No. I really think this is it. I am ready. Ready to give away my Precious Gift. Ready for the Big S.

Which is why I said to Michael, as he was getting ready to leave, 'Don't make any plans for tomorrow night. I have a surprise for you.'

And Michael was all, 'Really? What is it?'

But I said, 'If I told you, it wouldn't be a surprise, would it?'

And Michael just smiled and said, 'OK,' and kissed me again and said goodnight.

And left.

Oh, he's going to be surprised all right.

And I *know* that technically Michael and I making love is illegal since at sixteen I am still one year away from the age of consent in the state of New York.

I also realize that deciding to make love to my boyfriend two years before I actually planned to just because I don't want him to move to Japan and because I think there is a very strong possibility that he won't go if he knows he has access to free sex whenever he wants is manipulative and anti-feminist.

But I DON'T CARE.

I CAN'T let him move to Japan. I just CAN'T. I am very sorry for all the open-heart-surgery patients who may suffer because of this very selfish decision on my part.

But sometimes a girl has to do what a girl has to do just to stay sane in a topsy-turvy world where one minute you're eating cold sesame noodles, and the next minute your boyfriend is leaving for Japan.

That's just how it's going to have to be.

Oh, my God. I can't believe I'm doing this. Should I do this? SHOULD I DO THIS????

As usual, asking questions of my journal is no help whatsoever. I don't even know why I bother.

ME, A PRINCESS???? YEAH, RIGHT
A Screenplay by
Mia Thermopolis
(first draft)

Scene 16

INT/DAY – The Penthouse Suite at the Plaza Hotel. A scary-looking old woman with tattooed eyeliner (THE DOWAGER PRINCESS CLARISSE) is glaring at MIA, who cowers across from her in a chair. A hairless miniature poodle (ROMMEL) shivers nearby.

>   DOWAGER PRINCESS CLARISSE
> Now, let's see if I have this right:
> your father tells you that you are the
> Princess of Genovia, and you burst into
> tears. Why is this?

>   MIA
> I don't want to be a princess. I just
> want to be me, Mia.

>   DOWAGER PRINCESS CLARISSE
> Sit up straight in that chair. Do not
> drape your legs over the arm. And you are
> not Mia. You are Amelia. Are you telling
> me you have no wish to assume your
> rightful place upon the throne?

MIA

Grandmere, you know as well as I do
that I'm not princess material. So
why are we even wasting our time?

DOWAGER PRINCESS CLARISSE

You are the heir to the crown of
Genovia. And you will take my son's
place on the throne when he dies.
This is how it is. There is no other
way.

MIA

Yeah, whatever, Grandmere. Look,
I got a lot of homework. Is this
princess thing going to take long?

Thursday, September 9, Homeroom

I'm going to do it. I mean, Do It. Tonight. I was up all night thinking about it, and I know now – this is the only way.

I know it's selfish. I know I will be keeping a Shining Beacon of Hope from all the many heart patients Michael could be helping with his invention.

But that is just too bad for them. Plenty of people have had open-heart surgery and were just fine. Look at David Letterman. And Bill Clinton. People are just going to have to suck it up. Maybe if they ate less meat they wouldn't NEED open-heart surgery. Did anyone think of that?

Oh, God. Did I really just write that? I can't believe I just wrote that. WHAT'S HAPPENING TO ME? I'm becoming one of those militant vegetarians, the ones that think the Heifer Project, an organization that gives cows and goats to poor widows so they will have an income from selling the milk and be able to buy food for their children, is bad because it enslaves animals.

I don't know what's happening to me. It's like I've gone mental. I even checked to make sure I still had my condoms left over from when we were forced to go buy them during Health and Safety as part of our Safer Sex project. Of course, I made my selections on the basis of colour. I mean, there were just SO MANY to choose from. I knew I should have gone to Duane Reade and not Condomania. I have strawberry and pina colada in my backpack right now (I didn't realize the ones I bought were FLAVOURED until I checked their expiry dates this morning. Thank heaven they're still good).

GALWAY COUNTY LIBRARIES

I am willing to sacrifice my virginity for the sake of keeping my love in the same hemisphere as me.

But I just realized that during the course of this I may actually have to Touch It.

For the first time, however, this prospect is not making me say, or even think, the word *Ew*.

I must be maturing.

GALWAY COUNTY LIBRARIES

Thursday, September 9, Intro to Creative Writing

Describe a person you know:

His hair, at first glance, appears merely dark, but upon closer inspection is actually many strands of chestnut brown, gold and black. He wears it long, for a guy, not because doing so is 'in', but because he's too busy with his many interests to remember to get it cut regularly. His eyes seem dark at first glance as well, but are actually a kaleidoscope of russets and mahoganies, flecked here and there with ruby and gold, like twin lakes during an Indian summer, into which you feel as if you could dive and swim forever. Nose: Aquiline. Mouth: Eminently kissable. Neck: Aromatic – an intoxicating blend of Tide from his shirt collar, Gillette shaving foam and Ivory soap, which together spell: My boyfriend.

B-

Better I would have liked more description on what exactly it is about his mouth you find so Eminently kissable.

K. Martinez

101

Thursday, September 9, English

Now the big question is: Do I tell Tina?

I mean, obviously I can't tell *Lilly*. She'll see right through my plan and know what I'm trying to do. Which is not expressing my undying love and devotion for her brother, but trying to control him.

With sex.

I highly doubt she'd approve.

Plus she'll totally accuse me of violating the feminist code by using feminine wiles instead of my brain as a means to get what I want.

But isn't that what Gloria Steinem did when she went undercover as a sex kitten to expose the poor wages and long hours of the Playboy Bunnies, helping to improve their working conditions in the Grotto? I'm doing the same thing, basically. I am sacrificing my virginity in order to keep a valuable asset of our community from leaving it for a far off shore. In the long run, my sleeping with Michael tonight will only benefit the US economy.

You could almost say it's my duty as a citizen to Do It.

On the other hand, if Lilly and J.P. really did consummate their relationship over the summer (although I have been observing them both closely at lunch, the only period we all three share together and, beyond the Yodel exchange, I have seen no overt signs of shared intimacy. They don't even hold hands in the hallway or kiss when they see each other in the morning. Which may just be because they save all the lovey-dovey stuff for when they're alone together. OR it may be because they haven't got as far, intimacy-wise, as rumour would have it), Lilly ought to totally understand.

I mean, hormones are VERY POWERFUL things. It's not easy to fight them. Surely Lilly of all people would understand.

Except, of course, if you give up fighting them for the Wrong Reason.

Mia - what are you doing? Are you taking notes? I thought you'd read Franny and Zooey already!

No, Tina. I'm not taking notes. I'm writing in my journal. Tina, I have something to ask you. But I'm scared you might hate me for it.

I could never hate you! Besides, anything is better than listening to her going on about Salinger's fusion of Judaeo-Christian and Eastern religions.

Well, here's the thing: I don't think I'm going to be one of the Last Virgins at AEHS after tonight.

WHAT??? YOU AND MICHAEL ARE GOING TO DO IT!!!! OH, MIA!!!! WHEN DID YOU TWO DECIDE THIS?????

Well, WE didn't decide it. I decided it. Don't hate me, OK? But Grandmere gave me the key to the suite she's not using over at the Ritz, and I'm going to take Michael there tonight and surprise him.

You mean you're going to make sweet tender love to him so he'll have a beautiful memory to carry with him as he heads halfway across the world in order to prove himself worthy of you? Mia, that is SO ROMANTIC!!!!!!

Um, actually I was going to make sweet tender love to him so he'd change his mind and stick around New York. Because what guy is going to move to Japan if he can get regular sex right in his own neighbourhood?

Oh. Well. That's good too. I guess.

Seriously? You don't think I'm evil for trying to manipulate him emotionally? Using my Precious Gift?

Well, I understand why you're doing it. I mean, you love him, and so naturally, you don't want to lose him. And I know Boris didn't help at lunch yesterday, when he said all that stuff about clarinettists. Although truthfully, Mia, I highly doubt Michael is going to run into any clarinettists in Japan.

Still, I'm not sure I can risk it, Tina. I've got to do SOMETHING. I've got to TRY.

Right. But are you REALLY ready to go All The Way? I mean, have you been practicing with the shower head, like we learned how to do that night we saw *The 40 Year Old Virgin* on pay-per-view?

Of course! That movie was SOOOOO educational.

Right. And I mean, according to that movie, the whole thing should only take about one minute, given that this will be Michael's first time.

Yes, but then according to that movie, the second time should take TWO HOURS.

It took me that long the first time with the shower head. But I think it was because I was thinking about the wrong person. I was thinking about Boris, but later I figured out it works much better if I think about Cole from *Charmed*.

Me too! I mean, about the two hours. But James Franco from *Tristan + Isolde*, not Cole.

Do you think it's going to work in real life? I mean, without water?

I don't know, Tina. But it's a risk I'm willing to take, if it will mean keeping Michael by my side.

I totally understand. And I am with you a hundred per cent. You have condoms?

Of course. And I'm stopping by CVS after school for some contraceptive sponges. Because you know condoms alone are only like ninety-five per cent effective against preventing pregnancy if used correctly. I can't risk that extra five per cent.

But what's Lars going to say when he sees you buying contraceptive sponges? He's going to know they aren't for a class, like the condoms were. He takes all the same classes as you do - even if he doesn't exactly pay attention in them (then again . . . neither do you)!

I'm going to tell Lars they're a joke present for you. So play along, OK?

Ha. Ha ha. A joke present for me. That's really funny.

Well, I can't say they're a joke present for Lilly, because what if Lars asks her????

You aren't telling Lilly about this?

Tina, how can I? You know what she'll say.

That if Michael doesn't go to Japan, then his robotic surgical arm will never get made, and thousands of people will die who might not have done if you had just let him go?

Ouch, Tina. That really hurt.

I mean, I'm just saying that's what LILLY would say. I don't really BELIEVE that. At least, not very much. Michael is a very resourceful person. I'm sure he'll find a way to make his robotic surgical arm here. It's just that . . . did I mention my dad is on medication now for high blood pressure and high cholesterol, and his doctor says if he doesn't cut back his red-meat intake he's a prime candidate for bypass surgery?

Well, tell your mom to stop letting him order so much orange beef from Wu Liang Ye.

Yeah. I will. Oh, Mia! This is so exciting! You're going to be the first one in our group to give up her Precious Gift! Except Lilly, of course, if she and J.P. really Did It over summer break.

And you're *sure* you don't hate me for it? I mean, that I'm not waiting until the night of our senior prom, like we agreed?

Oh, Mia, of course not. I understand that there are mitigating circumstances. I mean, if Boris was offered first chair in some orchestra in Australia and was seriously considering going, I would do the exact same thing. Except of course Boris playing first chair at the Sydney Philharmonic isn't going to save anybody's life, let alone prove him worthy to a nation over which I might one day rule.

Thanks, Tina. I really mean that. Your support means a lot to me.

That's what I'm here for!

Really, could there BE a better friend than Tina Hakim Baba? I don't think so.

OK, so:

LIST OF THINGS TO DO BEFORE HAVING SEX:

1) Get contraceptive sponges
2) Shave underarms/legs
3) Shave bikini area????
4) Find fancy lingerie (do I OWN any fancy lingerie? Oh, there's that lavender silk teddy and tap pants from La Perla that Grandmere got me for my birthday. They still have the tags on them. I hope I don't get a rash from wearing them without washing them first)
5) Deodorant
6) Check for unsightly blackheads
7) Ditch Lars (easy. I will just tell him I am going to Michael's apartment for the evening and that he can come back and pick me up at eleven. Then Michael and I will sneak out down the back stairs and leave through the basement of the building. And we can take a cab up to the Ritz. Michael might get suspicious but I can just tell him it's part of the surprise)
8) EXFOLIATE!
9) Jolene moustache
10) Feed Fat Louie

Thursday, September 9, Lunch

So today when I got to the caff I found that someone had placed, on each and every lunch table, little triangular table-toppers that had all these warnings written on them. Like the one on our table said:

WARNING

Did you know that the single most likely-to-occur crisis currently facing Americans is a pandemic? With bioterrorism a real threat, and air travel as popular as it is today, deadly diseases such as avian flu and smallpox could erupt in our population at ANY time. Would YOU know what to do in the event of a bioterror attack?

PRINCESS MIA OF GENOVIA DOES.

Vote for a REAL LEADER.

Vote SMART.

Vote for Mia.

One on a nearby table said:

WARNING

Did you know that if a dirty bomb (an explosive device containing radioactive material inside it) went off in Times Square during school hours, even a mild wind could blow contaminated air our way in matter of minutes, causing radiation poisoning leading to cancer and/or death? Would

YOU know what to do in the event of a dirty-bomb attack?

PRINCESS MIA OF GENOVIA DOES.

Vote for a REAL LEADER.

Vote SMART.

Vote for Mia.

And on the next table, one that said:

WARNING

Did you know that in 1737 and again in 1884, New York City was rocked by estimated 5.0 earthquakes? The city is MORE than due for another one, and considering that much of lower Manhattan sits on sediment excavated from the World Trade Center when it was first built, and that most buildings here on the Upper East Side were built before earthquake-mitigating building codes were required, what are our chances of survival if a 5.0 or greater earthquake hit during school hours? Would YOU know what to do in the event of such a catastrophe?

PRINCESS MIA OF GENOVIA DOES.

Vote for a REAL LEADER.

Vote SMART.

Vote for Mia.

You didn't exactly have to be a REAL LEADER to figure out where these cheery little placards had come from. The minute I saw her coming towards our table, her tray piled high with salad and skinless chicken (Lilly has been trying to eat healthier lately. She's already lost ten pounds and looks much less like a pug than she used to. You can almost see her cheekbones), I went, 'What do you think you're doing?' and pointed at the table-topper.

'Cool, huh?' she said. 'J.P. ran them off on his dad's printer at his office.'

'No,' I said. 'Not cool. Lilly, what are you trying to do? SCARE people into voting for me?'

'Exactly,' Lilly said sitting down. 'That's the only thing these kids understand. They've been raised on Fox News and sensationalist journalism. They wouldn't know a real issue if one smacked them in the face. All they understand is fear. That's how we're going to win their votes.'

'Lilly,' I said. I couldn't believe this. 'I don't WANT people to vote for me because they're scared they won't know what to do in the event of a dirty-bomb attack if they don't. I want them to vote for me because they agree with my values and support my stand on the issues.'

'But you have no stand on any issues,' Lilly said, reasonably. 'You're going to step down if you win, anyway. So what do you care?'

'It's just . . .' I shook my head. 'I don't know. It seems wrong somehow.'

'Everyone else in politics and the media is doing it,' Lilly said. 'Why shouldn't we?'

'That doesn't make it any less wrong.'

'Hey.' J.P. set his tray down across from Lilly's. 'Do

you guys know what would happen if a Category Three or higher hurricane hit New York City? Don't laugh, it's happened before, in 1893 a mere Category One hurricane destroyed Hog Island, a resort island off the Rockaways in Queens. A whole ISLAND, with hotels on it and everything, and it disappeared overnight. Think about what a higher category hurricane could do. Would you know what to do in the event of such a disaster?' He pulled a table-topper from his pocket. 'Well, don't worry. Princess Mia of Genovia does.'

'Very funny,' I said to him. 'Lilly, seriously—'

'Mia, seriously,' Lilly said back to me. 'You just worry about how you're going to keep my brother from moving to Japan, and let me worry about your campaign for student-body president.'

I blinked at her. Wait. Lilly KNOWS??? HOW COULD SHE KNOW?????

She must have noticed my astonishment, since she rolled her eyes and went, 'Oh, please, POG. We've been best friends since first grade. You think I don't know how you operate by now? I'm sure whatever it is you're planning will be highly entertaining, if completely ineffective. But the boy's got his mind made up. You might as well surrender the fantasy.'

'Mia!' Ling Su hurried up to our table, looking panicky. 'Is it true? Is there really a chlorine-manufacturing plant in Kearny, New Jersey, that, if attacked by terrorists, could send a noxious cloud of chlorine gas over Manhattan that will kill or sicken us almost instantaneously?'

'What about an explosion at the Indian Point nuclear-power plant?' Perin wanted to know. 'Could the radiation plume really move south towards us and taint the city's water supply, killing thousands and making the city uninhabitable for decades?'

I glared at Lilly. 'Look what you've done!' I cried. 'You've freaked everybody out about stuff that could never happen!'

'What do you mean, stuff that could never happen?' Lilly demanded. 'What about that blackout? For years people were saying there could never be another blackout, but there WAS one. We were just lucky they got the power turned back on so quickly, or people would have started looting and killing one another for diapers.'

'Do you really know what to do in the event of a smallpox attack?' Ling Su asked me. 'Because the United States only has three hundred million doses stockpiled, and if you aren't one of the first people in line to get one, you'll probably die of it while you're waiting to get vaccinated. Do you have access to some secret stockpile because you're a princess or something? Can't you just get us the vaccinations now so that if a terrorist releases some smallpox into the air tomorrow or whatever, we'll be all right?'

'Lilly!' I was so disgusted I could hardly stand it. 'You've got to stop! See what you're doing? You're making people think I have access to a secret stockpile of smallpox vaccine and that if they vote for me I'll give them some! And it's not true!'

Ling Su and Perin looked disappointed to hear I didn't have smallpox vaccines at my beck and call. Boris, meanwhile, was laughing.

'What's so funny?' I demanded.

'Just –' He noticed Tina giving him the evil eye, so he stopped laughing. 'Nothing.'

'Look, POG,' Lilly said. 'I realize we're going for the

lowest common denominator here, but take a look around.'

I looked around the caff. Everywhere I glanced, people were picking up the table-toppers and talking about them – and darting nervous glances at me.

'See?' Lilly shrugged. 'It's working. People are falling for it. They're going to vote for you because they think you've got all the answers. And seriously, if Indian Point DID explode, what WOULD you do?'

'Make sure everyone had potassium iodide tablets to take within a few hours of exposure to help protect them from absorbing radiation. Insure that everyone had at least a few weeks' supply of clear water, canned food and prescription drugs so that they could stay inside with the ventilation off until the all clear,' I replied automatically.

'And in the event of an earthquake?'

'Take cover in a doorway or under a sturdy piece of furniture. After the initial shock, turn off all water, electricity and gas.'

'And if there's an avian flu outbreak?'

'Well, obviously everyone would need to start taking Tamiflu immediately, plus washing their hands and wearing disposable surgical masks while also staying away from pay phones, handrails and large crowds, such as at Macy's white sales and the 6 train at rush hour.'

Lilly looked triumphant. 'See? I wasn't making it up. You DO know what to do in the event of just about any potential crisis or disaster. I know this because you, Mia, are a worrier, and are therefore perhaps the single most disaster-prepared person in Manhattan. Don't try to deny it. We've all just witnessed the proof.'

I was pretty much speechless after that. I mean, while everything Lilly had just said was undeniably true, it still seemed wrong to me somehow. I mean, scaring the freshmen like that. Before lunch was over, three of them had come over to ask what I would do in the event of a dirty-bomb attack (instruct everyone to stay inside, then, once allowed to leave the area, make them remove, bag and dispose of their clothing before entering their homes, then wash immediately with soap and water), or a hurricane (duh: evacuate. With your cat).

Maybe Lilly really IS right though. In these uncertain times, it's possible that what people are really looking for is a leader who has already worried about and planned for these things, so they themselves don't have to worry and can be free to have fun.

Maybe that is why I was put on this planet – not to be Princess of Genovia, but so that I can worry about everything so nobody else has to bother.

Thursday, September 9, G and T

Lilly just showed me the going-away present she got for her brother: A Magic – The Gathering carrying case, so he can take his cards with him to Japan without getting them all messed up.

I didn't have the heart to tell her that

a) Michael doesn't play Magic any more, and
b) he won't be going to Japan, because I am planning on giving him a very, very good reason to stay right here in Manhattan.

Well, it wasn't that I didn't have the heart to tell her. I didn't tell her because I don't want her to kick my ass. She's been working out (which has also contributed to her weight loss) at Crunch, doing spin classes and also Ayurveda with her mom. Anyone who is willing to let a total stranger rub their nude body with oil and attars is someone whose bad side I do NOT want to get on.

Speaking of which, I have to remember to exfoliate before tonight.

It's sort of strange that I'm not more nervous and all. But I guess that just means I feel good about this decision. It just seems . . . right.

On a restaurant menu, there are four appetizers, five main courses and three desserts. How many different dinners can be ordered if each dinner consists of one appetizer, one main course and one dessert?

What about drinks? Did anyone think about THAT?

What, are the diners supposed to die of dehydration? Who WROTE this book anyway?

The price of jeans went up by thirty per cent since last year. If last year's price was x, what is this year's price in terms of x?

Oh my God, who CARES?

The average height (arithmetic mean) of four members of a six member cheerleading squad is 175 cm. What does the average height in centimetres of the other two cheerleaders have to be if the average height of the entire squad equals 180 cm?

CHEERLEADERS???? ON THE SATS?????

Oh my God, who am I fooling? I can't do this. I CANNOT DO THIS!!! I can't have SEX. I'm a PRINCESS, for crying out loud.

Oh my God, I think I'm having a heart attack.

OK. Well, this isn't embarrassing, or anything. I mean, that I hyperventilated during our PE class's run around the reservoir.

I am supposed to be breathing into a paper bag with my head between my knees. But I did that already and it didn't help. Well, obviously, I can breathe now. But I'm still FREAKING OUT. I can't believe I'm really going to DO IT.

What if something goes wrong and my mom and dad find out somehow? Like what if it turns out I still have my hymen or whatever (even though in Health and Safety last year they said that most girls lose theirs through ordinary physical activity, such as biking and horseback riding) and I start bleeding, and Michael has to rush me to Cabrini and some Dr-Kovac type has to put in a central line and then I slip into a coma like on *ER*?

EVERYONE WILL KNOW I GAVE AWAY MY PRECIOUS GIFT.

And OK, I have never actually heard of this happening to a girl, but in Tina's historical romance novels sometimes the girl does bleed – although she never seems to mind and goes on to have a massive earth-shattering orgasm anyway.

I just don't think I'm good enough at orgasms yet to have one under those particular circumstances. Particularly with someone else in the same room. Someone besides James Franco dressed in a suit of armour, I mean.

Oh no, here comes the nurse . . .

OK, well, Nurse Lloyd just said it's highly unlikely

118

anyone would bleed so much from the breaking of a hymen that they would have to be hospitalized, unless they are a haemophiliac. And she said that most women's hymens are already perforated. If they weren't, we wouldn't be able to menstruate.

So that whole Precious Gift thing is kind of bull.

She also said romance novels aren't necessarily the most reliable health guides and gave me a pamphlet that says *So You Think You're Ready For Sex.* The pamphlet has a confused-looking couple on the front and talks about the need for protection. It didn't say anything about your virginity being your Precious Gift that you should save for the person you marry. But it did say how you should wait to have sex until you have really got to know the person and are sure you really love them – which I already knew from the oxytocin thing.

And then there was some stuff about the age of consent (whatever. Like my dad would really press charges. Would he want the whole world to know his daughter had had premarital sex? Not so much), and not feeling pressured.

Then there was this section on abstinence and how it's OK *not* to Do It. Like this is supposed to be news to me. I fully know it's OK not to Do It. It's fine for other girls not to Do It.

But other girls' boyfriends have not invented robotic arms to use in heart surgery and are not moving to Japan for a year tomorrow.

I didn't say any of this stuff to Nurse Lloyd. Well, not the sex stuff. I told her about Michael though, and how he's moving and how I'm freaking out about it and am pretty sure I won't be able to survive if he actually leaves.

To which Nurse Lloyd replied, 'My brother had a triple bypass after a heart attack last year. They had to crack his chest open. He said he's never felt pain like that in his life, and that for six weeks afterwards he just wished he was dead.'

Which is very sad for Nurse Lloyd's brother, but in no way helps me out with MY problem.

Thursday, September 9, Chemistry

Mia, are you all right? I heard you spent PE in the nurse's office.

God, word travels fast in this school. And I'm fine thanks, J.P. Just got a little winded from running around the reservoir.

Got it. I'm glad you're all right. Though you look a little pale.

I have a lot on my mind, I guess.

That's right! Michael leaves tomorrow, right.

Yeah. Well, supposedly.

What do you mean, supposedly? I thought he was going for sure.

Well, maybe. We'll see.

It would be a shame if he didn't get to go. It's such a great opportunity.

I know it is. For him. But what about ME? I'm the one who's going to be stuck back here with nothing.

What do you mean with nothing? You've got ME!

Ha, ha. You know what I mean.

Well, I guess I sort of did wonder about that thing Boris said the other day at lunch. I know you got mad at him, but he did have a point . . . ARE you going to date other people while Michael's gone? I mean, have you two talked about that? Because it would be kind of unfair for him to expect you not to go out the whole time he's gone. I mean, with other guys. That is, if you wanted to.

But I don't want to!!!! I mean, I love Michael.

Of course you do. But you're also only sixteen years old. Are you really going to stay home every Saturday night until he gets back?

I don't have to stay home every Saturday night. I mean, I've got all my girls. L.O.V.E. and all that. Girls for life.

Your girls all have significant others. I'm not saying they won't want to spend time with you, but it's going to be kind of lonely when they're all out with their partners and you're home.

That's true. But it will be give me the opportunity to work on my novel. And my screenplay! And then maybe – if Michael really does go – I'll have them both done by the time he gets back. And then I'll have accomplished something too! Maybe not as earth-shattering as HIS accomplishment. But, you know. SOMETHING more than just being a princess.

I thought we established yesterday that just being you is enough of an accomplishment.

Yeah, but you were just being nice. Anybody can be THEMSELVES. I want to do something really special.

Mia, if you're not going to pay attention in this class, I don't see how you plan to pass it. Don't expect me to bail you out again this year, I've got other things to do — Kenny

That guy is really getting on my nerves.

He's right though. We should stop. It's wrong.

But it feels so right!

J.P.! Stop it! You're making me laugh!

Good. You need a laugh, I suspect.

J.P. is so nice!!!! Lilly's so lucky to have found such a perfect guy.

All right, back to Chemistry.

Wait . . . there's HOW many chemical compounds? And we have to know them ALL???????

Thursday, September 9, Pre-Calculus

Reasons To Do It Tonight v Wait Until Prom Night

Pro:
It could convince him to stay in New York and not move to Japan, thus keeping me from having a nervous breakdown when he isn't around for me to smell his neck.

Con:
It could convince him to stay in New York and not move to Japan, thus depriving the world of a potentially life-saving medical breakthrough, and my grandmother of her reason to keep trying to fix me up with other guys she believes are 'more worthy' (meaning richer) than Michael.

Pro:
Michael says he is never going to another prom anyway, so I might as well·just get it over with now.

Con:
But maybe by the time my senior prom rolls around, he might be so desperate for sex he'll agree to go after all!

Pro:
It will be a chance for us to express our love physically in a way that will truly make us one heart, one mind, one soul.

Con:
What if I pass gas or something? I mean, seriously, you are NAKED, he's going to be able to tell it was you.

Pro:

Speaking of naked, I will finally get to see Michael naked.

Con:

He will get to see ME naked.

Pro:

By having sex tonight, instead of waiting until prom night, we will avoid being a cliché like couples in teen movies.

Con:

The fact that I am not yet eighteen could lead to legal complications for Michael down the road. Although I'm sure my dad wouldn't want the tabloids finding out about something like that.

Pro:

Lilly's Done It already. At least I think so. And it doesn't seem to have done her and J.P. any harm.

Con:

I don't actually know this for sure.

Pro:

By giving each other the Precious Gift of our virginity, we will be forging an emotional and spiritual bond with one another that we will never have with anyone else in our lives, even if the unthinkable should happen and we some day part ways.

Con:
I can't think of a con to that one.

Oh whatever. We're so Doing It.
I'm so going to throw up.

Homework

Homeroom: N/A
Intro to Creative Writing: Some idiotic thing I can't remember
English: 1000 words on *Raise High the Roof Beam, Carpenter*
French: More *décrire un soir amusant avec les amis*
G and T: N/A
PE: N/A
Chemistry: Who knows?
Pre-Calculus: Who cares?

Only six more hours until Michael and I Do It!!!!!!!!

Thursday, September 9, the Four Seasons

It's getting harder and harder to find Grandmere for my princess lessons these days. We finally tracked her down in the penthouse of the Four Seasons, but when I walked in it was bedlam, as usual.

'These curtains are unacceptable,' Grandmere was saying to a man in a business suit whose gold name tag read Jonathan Greer.

'I'll have them replaced immediately, madam,' Jonathan Greer said.

Grandmere looked kind of surprised that he wasn't arguing. She said, 'A floral print. NOT stripes.'

'Absolutely, madam,' Jonathan Greer said. 'They'll be replaced with floral patterned curtains at once.'

Grandmere gave him a startled look. She was clearly used to more resistance from the hotel concierges she's been dealing with lately.

'And I cannot abide leather furniture,' she said, pointing to a very nice club chair in the corner. 'It's far too slippery and Rommel dislikes it. The smell makes him nervous. He was kicked in the head by a cow once.'

'I'll have the chair recovered at once, madam,' the concierge said. He caught my eye, and nodded politely in my direction. But then he turned back to Grandmere. 'Perhaps in the same material as the curtains?'

Grandmere looked even more taken aback. 'Why, yes . . . yes, that would be acceptable.'

'And would Your Highness care for tea,' Jonathan Greer wanted to know, 'as I see your granddaughter has arrived? Service for two can be brought immediately. Finger sandwiches or scones or both?'

Grandmere looked like she might pass out, she was so

astonished. 'Both, of course,' she said. 'And Earl Grey tea.'

'Absolutely,' Jonathan Greer said, as if there were no other kind. 'And perhaps a cocktail for you, Your Highness? I believe a Sidecar – served in a stemmed cocktail glass, no sugar on the rim – is your preference?'

Grandmere had to sit down. She did it gracefully – well, except for the part where she almost sat on Rommel. But he got out of the way in the nick of time. It's not like he hasn't had plenty of practice.

'That would be lovely,' she said faintly.

'Anything that we can do to make your stay in the Royal Suite more pleasurable, Your Highness,' Jonathan Greer said with a bow. 'You need only call.'

And with that, he stepped smartly out of the room and into the hallway – where I saw my dad, out of Grandmere's sight, slip the guy a folded up bill and murmur his thanks.

Wow. My dad can be slick sometimes.

'So,' he said to Grandmere as he strolled back into the room. 'What do you think? Does this place meet with your approval?'

'It's called the Royal Suite,' Grandmere said, still a bit faintly.

'Indeed it is,' my dad said. 'Three bedrooms of luxury for you, Rommel and your maid. I hope you approve. Look . . . there's even an ashtray.'

Grandmere blinked at the crystal bowl he held up. 'There are roses,' she said. 'Pink and white. In vases everywhere.'

'Well, look at that,' Dad said. 'So there are. Do you think you can stand to live here until your condo at the Plaza is completed?'

Grandmere rallied herself. 'I suppose it will be *tolerable*,' she said. 'Though hardly what I'm used to.'

'Of course not,' Dad said. 'But sometimes in life we must suffer. Mia. How are you?'

I jumped away from the window, which I'd been looking out of. We were on the thirty-second floor, and I have to say that the view, while beautiful, wasn't doing much for the vomity feeling I was kind of pushing down.

I didn't just feel like throwing up either. There was fluttering going on in my stomach. It was like there was one of those hummingbirds that sometimes hover around outside my window in Genovia trapped inside my abdomen.

I'm sure this was just nervous anticipation of the ecstasy I am bound to experience tonight in Michael's arms.

'I'm fine,' I said to my dad. Too fast though, since he gave me a strange look.

'Are you sure?' he asked. 'You look . . . pale.'

'I'm good,' I said. 'Just, um, ready for today's princess lesson!'

My dad gave me an even STRANGER look at that. I have NEVER been ready for a princess lesson. EVER.

'Oh, Amelia,' Grandmere groaned from her couch. 'I haven't the time or patience today. Jeanne and I have so much unpacking to do.' Which translates from Grandmere speech to *My maid Jeanne has to unpack while I, the Dowager Princess, boss her around.* 'I need to get settled before I can think of more things to teach you. This constant moving about has been VERY unsettling. Not just for me, but for Rommel as well.'

We all looked at Rommel, who had curled into a ball

at the end of the couch and was snoring fitfully, while he dreamed of being far, far away from Grandmere.

'Well, Mother,' Dad said. 'Now that you have Mr Greer looking after you, I feel as if I can leave you for a bit –'

Grandmere just snorted. 'Which lucky Victoria's Secret lingerie model is it tonight, Philippe?' she wanted to know. Then, before he could even answer, she went on to say, 'Amelia, all this rushing around town has wreaked havoc on my pores. I'm going to have a facial. Princess lessons are cancelled for the day.'

'Um,' I said. 'OK, Grandmere.' It was really hard to hide my relief. I have a LOT of shaving to do.

Hmmm, I wonder if she knows this, and that's WHY she's letting me go home early?

But no, that's not possible. Not even GRANDMERE could actually WANT me to have premarital sex.

But wait. Why else would she have given me that key?

No. Not even Grandmere could be that calculating.

Could she?

Thursday, September 9, the Moscovitzes' Apartment, 7 p.m.

OK, so I'm here. I'm shaved and exfoliated and conditioned; the sponges are secured in my backpack and I think I'm ready.

I mean, aside from the throwing-up feeling, which still hasn't gone away.

Everything is *crazy* here. Michael is packing to leave and his mother seems to think they don't actually have things like shampoo and toilet paper in Japan. She keeps slipping that kind of stuff into his suitcase. She and Maya, the Moscovitzes' housekeeper, went to Sam's Club in New Jersey and bought a year's supply of stuff like family-sized containers of Tums for him to take with him.

He's like, 'Mom, I'm sure they have Tums in Japan. Or something similar. I do not need a family-sized container of them. Or this giant vat of Listerine mouthwash.'

But Dr Moscovitz doesn't care, she just keeps putting them back in his suitcase every time Michael takes them out.

It's kind of sad. I mean, I know how Dr Moscovitz feels. She just wants to have SOME feeling of control in a world that is rapidly spinning into chaos. And apparently making sure her son has enough antacids to last him until the next millennium helps Michael's mother feel more in control.

I wish I could tell her she has nothing to worry about, since Michael won't be going to Japan after all. But I can't really let HER in on my plan before I let MICHAEL in on it.

Anyway, I already told him we're going to be sneaking out. He doesn't like it – he's always afraid of getting on my dad's bad side, which I can understand might be a concern to anyone, seeing as how my dad has command of an elite security task force – but I can tell he's intrigued. He was like, 'OK. Let me just find my jacket. I know it's in my room . . . somewhere.'

Little does he know he's not going to need his jacket.

Lilly just came out of her room with her video camera and was like, 'Oh good, POG, I'm glad you're here. Quick – what are some ways you'd reduce climate-heating pollution so that we don't experience a climatic disaster equivalent to the ones portrayed in *The Day After Tomorrow* and *Category 6*? I mean, if you ruled the world, and not just Genovia.'

'Lilly,' I said. 'I am not in the mood to be on your TV show right now.'

'This isn't for *Lilly Tells It Like It Is*, it's for the campaign. Come on, quick. Pretend you're addressing the Genovian Parliament.'

I sighed. 'Fine. Well, instead of spending three hundred billion dollars a year extracting and refining fossil fuels, I'd urge world leaders to spend that money developing alternative clean energy resources, like solar, wind and biofuels.'

'Good,' Lilly said. 'What else?'

'Is this part of your Scare-The-Freshmen-Into-Voting-For-Me thing?' I asked. 'Because I'm such a worrywart that I've already researched what to do in the event of most disasters?'

'Just answer the question.'

'I'd help developing nations, which are the ones causing the most pollution, to switch over to clean energy
resources too. And require auto makers to manufacture
only gas-electric hybrid cars, and buy back all SUVs, and
provide tax breaks to consumers and businesses that
switch from fossil-fuel burning to solar or wind power.'

'Awesome. Why do you look so funny?'

I put a hand up to my face. I'd been extra careful with
my make-up, because Michael would be seeing it up
extra close. I didn't want it to look like I was wearing
any. Boys like the natural look. Well, boys like Michael
anyway.

'What do you mean?' I asked. 'Funny how?' Was I getting a zit? That would be just my luck, right when my
boyfriend is totally going to be gazing into my eyes as he
makes love to me, for me to have a giant honking zit in
the middle of my forehead.

'No. You just look really nervous. Like you're going to
throw up.'

'Oh.' Thank God it wasn't a zit. 'I don't know what
you're talking about.'

'POG.' Lilly lowered the camera and stared at me
curiously. 'What's going on? What are you up to? What
are you and Michael doing tonight anyway? He said you
had some kind of surprise for him?'

Thank God Michael just came out of his room, carrying his denim jacket and going, 'Sorry, I'm ready now.'

I wish I could say the same.

Thursday, September 9, 8 p.m., the Ritz

Have to write fast – Michael is tipping the room-service guy. Everything is going perfectly . . . we got out of the building without anyone suspecting a thing. Michael doesn't like sneaking around – I think he believes my dad could have him killed by the Genovian Royal Guard with a single command (he couldn't really, they aren't allowed to kill anyone unless war has been declared), but has maintained an air of tolerant amusement – at least so far. He thinks we're just having a romantic good-bye dinner for two in my grandmother's abandoned hotel suite (which, thank God, they've cleaned since she left. I don't think I could go through with this if the place still reeked of Chanel No 5, as most rooms tend to after Grandmere's been there). He doesn't know I'm about to make him the recipient of my Precious Gift.

Ooooh, he's coming back. I will drop the bomb after dinner . . . the sex bomb, I mean.

Hey, isn't that the name of a song?

Thursday, September 9, 10 p.m., taxi home from the Ritz

I can't believe he –

Oh my God, how am I even going to write this down? I can't even THINK it, how can I WRITE it???? I really can't even SEE to write it, the light in here is so bad. I can only see the page when we're stopped in traffic under a street-lamp.

But since Ephraim Kleinschmidt – that's my cab driver's name, according to his licence in the bullet-proof screen between him and me – took Fifth Avenue and not Park, like I asked, we are stopped in traffic A LOT.

Which is good. No, really, it's GOOD. Since I guess it means I can hopefully get all my crying out of my system before we get to the Loft, so I don't have to face the Big Interrogation from Mom and Mr G when I walk in looking like Kirsten Dunst after the hot tub scene from *Crazy/Beautiful*. You know. Crying hysterically and all.

The crying is really freaking Ephraim Kleinschmidt out. I guess he's never had a sobbing sixteen-year-old princess in his cab before. He keeps on looking back here in his rear-view mirror and trying to hand me Kleenexes from the box on his dashboard.

As if Kleenex is going to help!!!!!

The only thing that's going to help is getting this down in some kind of lucid manner to help me make sense of it. Because it *makes no sense*. *None* of this makes any sense. It CAN'T be happening. It CAN'T.

Except that it is.

I just don't understand how he could never have

135

TOLD me. I mean, seriously, I thought we had a perfect relationship.

OK, maybe not PERFECT because no one has a PER-FECT relationship. I will admit the computer stuff really really bored me.

But at least he KNEW that and didn't go on about it. That much.

And I know the princess lessons stuff really bored him. I mean, the stuff about who to curtsy to when and all. So I tried to spare him too.

But other than that, I thought we had a good relationship. An OPEN relationship. A relationship where we could TELL each other things and didn't have any secrets.

I had no idea Michael has been keeping something like this from me the WHOLE TIME we've been going out.

And his excuse – that I never asked – is BOGUS. I'm sorry, but that is just – OH MY GOD, EPHRAIM KLEINSCHMIDT, NO I DO NOT WANT ANY KLEENEX – stupid. You don't NOT tell your girlfriend something like that, even if she never asked, because she just ASSUMED . . .

Although I should have known. I mean, what was I THINKING???? Michael is way too hot not to have –

OK. Lucid. Right.

Everything was going great. At least, I THOUGHT everything was going great. The throw-up feeling had even gone away. It's true I couldn't eat very much – I ordered the bluefin tuna two ways with artichoke salad with fava beans and scallions and parmesan shavings for me, and the chicken *à la moutarde*, fresh peas, cipollini onions, baby carrots and pea 'cappuccino' sauce for

Michael, plus milk chocolate mousse to share for dessert. I was kind of worried about the scallions but I had a Listerine Pocket Pak in my bag – because I was so nervous about what I knew I was about to do.

But just BEING with Michael and in the vicinity of his neck and therefore his pheromones calmed me down so much that by the time we got to the mousse, I felt like I really could go through with it.

So I went, summoning all my courage, 'Michael, remember that time my mom and Mr G went to Indiana and I got to stay in that hotel room at the Plaza and I invited Lilly and Tina and everyone to stay there with me and not you and you got so mad?'

'I didn't get mad,' Michael pointed out.

'Yeah, but you were disappointed I didn't invite YOU to stay in it with me.'

'That,' Michael said, 'is true.'

'Well, so, I have this hotel suite to myself now,' I said. 'And I invited you, and not Lilly and those guys.'

'You know,' Michael said, smiling. 'I'd sort of noticed that. But I didn't want to say anything, in case the girls were coming by after dinner.'

'Why would the girls come by after dinner?'

'That was a joke. I sort of figured they weren't. But with you it's kind of hard to predict sometimes.'

'Oh. Well, the thing is –' and it was SOOO hard for me to say this, but I HAD to do it. What's more, I WANTED to do it. I mean, I genuinely and truly felt like I was ready to Do It – 'I know I said I wanted to wait until my senior prom for us to have sex. But I've been giving it a lot of thought, and I really think I'm ready now. Tonight.'

Michael didn't look as shocked as I thought he would.

137

I think mostly because we had already snuck out behind my bodyguard's back and were already eating dinner by ourselves in a hotel room. Now that I think of it, all of that might have been a bit of a giveaway.

Then he said something that completely freaked me out (I didn't know then that it was just the FIRST of MANY things Michael was going to say that would totally freak me out).

'Mia,' he said. 'Are you sure about this? Because you were pretty firm on the whole prom-night thing, and I don't want you changing your mind just because I'm going away for a while and you're afraid I might, er, hook up with a geisha girl, like you mentioned before.'

!!!!!!!!!!!

Obviously, I was like, 'Um . . . what?'

Because, let's face it: Michael has been quite vocal in his desire for – well – me, over the past year. And the fact that he was even QUESTIONING my offer had me reeling.

Not to mention the part where he hadn't yet thrown me down on the bed and declared that he definitely wouldn't be going to Japan now.

'I know,' he said, looking as if he were in actual physical pain. 'It's just that . . . well, I don't want this to happen for the wrong reasons. Like because you think if we do this I'm going to change my mind about going or something.'

So then I just sat there blinking at him, because . . . well, because I couldn't believe this was happening!!!! I mean, that he was so willing to Do It and then take off anyway!!!!!! It was quite clear that he believed, as Tina

138

had initially, that I was only offering to make sweet tender love with him so he'd have a beautiful memory to carry with him as he headed halfway across the world in order to prove himself worthy of me.

Which, excuse me, but – NO. WAY.

'Um,' I said. Because I was so confused. 'No. That is not why I changed my mind about prom night. That is SO not why.'

'Really.' Michael TOTALLY looked as if he didn't believe me. 'So if we make love tonight, you are not going to be mad if I leave for Japan tomorrow?'

'No,' I said. I was sure my nostrils were flaring like crazy because I was telling such a whopper. But I hoped the lights were low enough that he wouldn't notice. 'But, I mean . . . I guess I have to say I'm kind of surprised you'd still WANT to go. Considering, you know. It's sex. With me. On what could be a regular basis.'

'Mia,' Michael said. 'I keep telling you – part of the reason I'm going is for US. So people like your grandmother will stop asking, "Why is she with HIM? She's a princess, and he's just some random guy she went to high school with."'

'I understand,' I said. I was trying to be way mature, but I have to admit I felt like crying. It wasn't just that he'd said he would still go to Japan even if we Did It. It was that . . . well, I sort of had the feeling we weren't actually going to Do It after all now, because truthfully the mood was kind of spoilt, and I was actually disappointed.

I mean, I guess I had been kind of looking forward to it. Throw-up feeling aside.

'I know that you feel like you have to prove you're worthy of me and all that,' I went on, hardly even knowing what I was saying, I was trying so hard to salvage the situation. Because I thought MAYBE there was a chance that if we actually went ahead and Did It after all, he'd change his mind afterwards. I mean, what if it was just that he didn't yet know what he was missing? 'And I know your robotic surgical arm is important. But I think WE'RE more important. OUR LOVE is more important. And I think giving one another the Precious Gift of our virginity would be the most powerful expression of our love ever.'

And Michael went, 'The precious WHAT?'

That is the thing about boys. They just don't KNOW anything. I mean, they know about Halo and html and robotic surgical arms, but important stuff? Not so much.

'The Precious Gift of our virginity,' I repeated. 'I think we should give it to each other. Now. Tonight.'

And then Michael said the thing that COMPLETELY and TOTALLY freaked me out. The other stuff – about how he planned on going to Japan tomorrow regardless of whether or not we had sex – was NOTHING compared to what Michael said next. Which was:

'Mia.' He looked at me like I was nuts. 'I gave my – what'd you call it? Oh yeah, my Precious Gift – away a long time ago.'

!!!!!!!!!!!!!!!!!

!!!!!!!!!!!!!!!!!

!!!!!!!!!!!!!!!!!

At first I just figured I had misunderstood him. I mean, because he was LAUGHING as he said it, like it was no big deal. Surely no one would LAUGH as they said they'd given away their Precious Gift. No one who meant it SERIOUSLY.

But when I just looked at him, Michael stopped laughing and went, 'Wait. What? Why are you looking at me like that?'

And this horrible cold feeling crept over me.

'Michael,' I said. It was as if someone had lowered the air conditioning in the room about ten degrees all of a sudden. 'Are you not a virgin?'

And he went, 'No, of course not. You know that.'

!!!!!!!!!!!!!!!!!!!!
....

To which of course I replied, 'NO, I DID NOT KNOW THAT' and, 'WHAT ARE YOU TALKING ABOUT?'

And Michael actually started to look alarmed. I guess because I yelled it so loud. But I didn't care. Because:

!!!!!!!!!!!!!!!!!!!
....

'Well,' he said. 'I guess we never actually TALKED about it, but I didn't think it was a big deal—'

'YOU HAVE HAD SEX BEFORE, AND YOU DIDN'T THINK THAT WAS A BIG DEAL??? A BIG ENOUGH DEAL TO TELL YOUR GIRLFRIEND????'

Seriously, I know it sounds lame, but I was about to cry. Because – his Precious Gift! He had given it to someone else! And never even thought it was a big enough deal to tell me about it!

'It was before you and I even started going out,' Michael said. He looked totally panicky now. Not that I cared. 'I didn't think – I mean, it was so long ago—'

'WHO?' I couldn't stop yelling. I wanted to. I knew I wasn't being cool. I'm sure this wasn't how Tina acted when Boris tearfully confessed about Lilly having Touched It.

But I genuinely couldn't help myself. 'WHO WAS IT?'

'Who'd I have sex with?' Michael kept blinking. 'I don't think I want to tell you. You might try to kill her or something. Your eyes are actually spinning around in their sockets a little bit right now.'

'WHO WAS IT??????'

'God, it was Judith, OK?' Michael had stopped looking scared. Now he just looked annoyed. 'What is WITH you? It didn't mean anything, we were just messing around. It was before I even knew you liked me, so what do you care?'

'Judith?' So many thoughts were colliding into each other inside my head, it was like the inside of my brain had turned into a giant demolition derby. 'JUDITH GERSHNER???? YOU HAD SEX WITH JUDITH GERSHNER???? YOU SAID YOU WERE JUST FRIENDS!!!!!!'

'We were!' Michael had stood up. So had I. We were standing across the room from each other, yelling. At least, I was yelling. Michael was just talking. 'But we were friends who messed around a little.'

'You told me you weren't going out with her! You told me she had a boyfriend!'

'I wasn't,' he insisted. 'And she did! But . . .'

'But WHAT?'

'But.' He shrugged. 'I don't know. We were just messing around. I TOLD YOU.'

'Oh, REALLY?' I couldn't believe this. I could not believe that Michael and Judith Gershner had – had – I mean, I've HUNG OUT with Judith Gershner. Well, not HUNG OUT with her, necessarily. But TALKED to her.

And the whole time I'd never had the slightest idea that SHE had carnal knowledge of my boyfriend. SHE had been the recipient of his Precious Gift. Not me. NEVER ME.

Because once you've given your gift away, you can't take it back and give it to someone else you might happen to like better, or even love. No. It says so right in Tina's book. It is GONE.

GONE.

'Did JUDITH feel that way?' I heard myself yelling. 'Did JUDITH think the two of you were just messing around? Or was she in love with you? Did she know she was giving you her Precious Gift just so you could turn around and start dating me?'

'First of all,' Michael said, 'if you don't stop saying *Precious Gift*, I'm going to hurl. Second of all, I told you, we were just messing around. Judith wasn't in love with me and I wasn't in love with her. I wasn't even her first, for crying out loud!'

I felt myself blanch. 'OH MY GOD. Did you use protection? What if she GAVE YOU SOMETHING?'

'She didn't give me anything! Of course I used protection! I don't understand what the big deal is. It's not like I cheated on you. This was before you even sent me those anonymous love poems. I didn't have the slightest idea you liked me. If I'd known—'

'If you'd known, WHAT?' I demanded. 'You wouldn't have given your Precious Gift to Judith?'

'I told you not to call it that. But yes, basically.'

'So it's MY fault?' I shrieked. 'It's my fault you lost

your virginity to someone other than me, because I was SHY????'

'I didn't say that.'

'You could have told me you liked me, you know, instead of sleeping with JUDITH GERSHNER!'

'What would have been the point?' Michael demanded. 'You were going out with Kenny Showalter at the time, if I recall.'

I gasped. 'BUT I DIDN'T LIKE HIM!'

'How was I supposed to know that? You claim you didn't like Josh Richter either, but you certainly talked about him enough.'

I gasped even louder. JOSH RICHTER? He had the nerve to bring up JOSH RICHTER? TO MY FACE?

'And you certainly hung out with Kenny enough,' Michael went on. 'I mean, for a guy you claim not to have liked. Which is fine – I don't care, because you came to your senses in the end. But don't get mad at me because you took your sweet time about admitting you liked me and I didn't wait around for you.'

'The way you're expecting me to wait around for you while you go off to Japan and find yourself?' I yelled.

Michael looked totally confused. 'This doesn't have anything to do with my going to Japan. What are you even *talking* about?'

'CLARINETTISTS!' I heard myself yell. I didn't mean to. I didn't WANT to. I was just so emotionally overwrought by everything I'd just heard, I couldn't stop myself. Once again, my mouth was going off without my brain to back up what it was saying. 'You're going off to Japan and you just expect me to wait around alone every Saturday until you get back. Well, what if I don't WANT to wait around alone for you? Did you ever think of THAT?'

'Mia.' Michael got very quiet suddenly. 'What are you saying?'

'I'm saying I'm only sixteen years old,' I burst out before I could stop myself. 'And you're going away for a year. OR MORE. And it's not fair of you to expect me just to sit home like a freaking nun while you're off with some Japanese CLARINETTIST!'

'Mia.' Michael shook his head. 'You've totally lost me with the clarinettist thing. I don't have the slightest idea what you're talking about. But so far as me expecting you to sit at home like a freaking nun – I never asked you to do that. I didn't exactly think you'd WANT to date other people while I'm gone – I certainly don't have the slightest intention of going out with other people while I'm gone – but if you want to, I guess it wouldn't exactly be fair of me to hold it against you. Except that I thought . . .' Whatever he was about to say, he seemed to think better of it. He shook his head. 'Never mind. Look, if that's what you want . . .'

Except that that WASN'T what I wanted!!!! That was the LAST THING I wanted.

But it didn't look as if I was going to get ANYTHING that I wanted. What I'd WANTED was for Michael and me to give each other our Precious Gifts – sorry, make love – tonight, and for him to say afterwards that he'd changed his mind and wasn't going to Japan tomorrow after all.

But it turned out he HAD no Precious Gift to give, and he also had no intention of staying in America, whether I slept with him or not.

I HAD COMPROMISED MY FEMINIST

145

PRINCIPLES BY OFFERING TO SLEEP WITH HIM NOW, TONIGHT, INSTEAD OF AFTER MY SENIOR PROM LIKE I HAD ALWAYS INSISTED, AND HE HAD BASICALLY SAID, 'NO, THANK YOU.'

Well, more or less.

Did he really think I was just going to FORGIVE him for that?

Which has to be why I just looked at him and went, 'Yes, Michael. That's EXACTLY what I want. Because the truth is, if you've kept something like this from me through our whole relationship, it just makes me wonder what kind of relationship we really even have. I mean, you haven't been HONEST with me –'

'YOU FREAKING NEVER ASKED!' Now HE was yelling. 'I didn't even know it was important to you! I don't even know where the hell this *Precious Gift* crap came from!'

But it was too late. Much too late.

'– and the fact that you're so willing to move to ANOTHER COUNTRY,' I went on, 'pretty much signals to me that this relationship has never meant all that much to you anyway.'

'Mia.' Michael shook his head. Just once. He wasn't yelling any more. 'Don't do this.'

But what else was I supposed to do? WHAT ELSE???

I reached up and undid the snowflake necklace from around my neck. The snowflake necklace he'd given me on my fifteenth birthday. I held it out to him, the way Arwen gave her necklace – the Evenstar – to Aragorn as a parting gift to remember her by as he attempted to regain his throne in an effort to win her father's approval.

146

Only I was giving Michael his necklace back – not because I wanted him to keep it to remember me by.

But because I didn't want it any more.

Because suddenly that snowflake was just a reminder of who ELSE had been at that dance – Judith Gershner.

And OK, she'd been there with another guy. That girl really seemed to get around. But still.

The thing is, it was totally different for Aragorn and Arwen. Because Aragorn never Did It with a girl who knew how to clone fruit flies. And then lied about it.

And OK, only by omission. But still.

He NEVER TOLD ME. What ELSE hasn't he told me???? HOW CAN I TRUST HIM WHEN HE GOES TO JAPAN????

'Mia,' Michael said, this time in a totally different voice. Not like he was choked up, like Aragorn had been. But like he wanted to punch me in the face. Which I knew he'd never do. But still. He looked pretty angry. 'Do. Not. Do. This.'

'Goodbye, Michael,' I said with a sob. Because WHAT ELSE WAS THERE TO SAY?

And I dropped the necklace on the floor – because he wouldn't take it – and ran out of there before I choked on my own tears.

And now Ephraim Kleinschmidt has pulled up in front of my building and wants seventeen dollars. I'm going to give him a twenty and let him keep the change as a tip. I owe him that much at least, for all the Kleenexes. Which I finally did start using, because I totally can't stop crying. There's no WAY I'm going to be able to hide what happened from my mom. If she's still up when I get inside, anyway.

If this is what self-actualization feels like, all I have

to say is, I was a lot happier before I became self-actualized.

Thursday, September 9, 11 p.m., the Loft

Mom was up.

I'm in bed now with a cool washcloth over my forehead. That's because when I walked into the loft and she looked away from *Law & Order* to ask me how my evening went, I had to run for the toilet, where I threw up my bluefin tuna two ways with artichoke salad with fava beans and scallions and parmesan shavings. Not to mention the chocolate mousse.

I've got her to promise not to call Dr Fung's emergency service. The only thing about me that's sick is my heart.

And I'm pretty sure Dr Fung doesn't have a prescription for what's wrong with it.

Thursday, September 9, 11.30 p.m., the Loft

Mom says she doesn't think Michael not telling me about losing his virginity to Judith Gershner is that big a deal – not worth breaking up with him over anyway. Her exact words were, 'Oh, Mia. It's just SEX.'

That's easy for her to say. She lost her virginity when she was younger than me, and to a guy who is now married to a former CORN PRINCESS. AND she's happily married to someone else. Of course it's just SEX to her. To me, it's my LIFE.

'Mom, he LIED to me,' I said.

'Well, he didn't EXACTLY lie,' Mom said. 'I mean, you asked him if he and Judith were going out. And they weren't.'

'Mom. GOING OUT implies sleeping together.'

'Since when?' Mom wanted to know. 'I thought HOOKING UP meant sleeping together. And you didn't ask Michael that. You asked him if he and Judith were GOING OUT.'

The reason we both know this is because I went back through my old diaries, just to make sure I was right.

And I was.

'Are you sure you didn't pick a fight with Michael over this because it's easier for you to cope with him being gone if you're mad at him than if you were still loving him and missing him all the time?' was her next totally off the wall question.

Yeah, right, Mom. Because I am feeling SO MUCH BETTER NOW.

I didn't tell her how the subject had come up. I mean, about HOW I'd found out about Michael and Judith. The last thing I need is my mom knowing what I'd tried

150

to do – you know, convince Michael not to go to Japan by sleeping with him. She wouldn't be TOO disappointed in me for being such a bad feminist and using sex as a manipulative tool or anything.

The phone just rang. I didn't even check the caller ID to see who it was, because I knew. Who else would call this late and risk waking up Rocky (who could sleep through a war protest . . . and actually has)?

And Mom confirmed it when she looked in to say it was Michael, saying sorry to call so late but I wasn't picking up my cell and he wanted to make sure I'd made it home OK.

Like I'll ever be OK again.

Mom asked if I wanted to speak to him and I just looked at her and she said, 'Um, Michael, now is probably not the best time,' into the phone and went away.

My chest feels funny. Like it's empty and hollow inside. I wonder if this is because I just barfed up the rest of my dinner or if it's because my heart has shattered into so many little pieces it's basically disappeared.

Thursday, September 9, 11.45 p.m.

Michael just emailed me:

SkinnerBx: Mia, I don't understand what just
happened. Judith Gershner is a nice
person, but she's never meant anything to me and never will. I don't
understand how the fact that I
slept with her three years ago,
BEFORE YOU AND I EVER WENT OUT, is
a valid reason for you and me
breaking up. If that's what just
happened, which, as I said, I'm not
even sure about, because you were
acting so weird.

And as for your thinking that I
expect you to wait for me while I'm
in Japan . . . well, yeah, I guess
I kind of thought you would, considering the fact that part of the
reason I'm going is to improve
the chances of our being able to
have a future together. Maybe
that's a lot to ask. Maybe I have
no right to expect it. I don't know.
I don't understand any of this.
Could you maybe call or write back
and possibly explain? Because I'm
totally clueless. And this is all so
stupid.

God. That is so like him. What is so stupid about my

wanting a boyfriend who actually VALUES intimacy and doesn't dismiss his first sexual experience as just 'messing around'?

And OK, she already had a boyfriend, apparently. That just makes it worse. He was messing around with a girl who was messing around with him BEHIND HER BOYFRIEND'S BACK.

And JUDITH GERSHNER???? How could he have had sex with JUDITH GERSHNER???? And not have TOLD me???? I mean, I have eaten LUNCH with Judith Gershner. I have gone ICE-SKATING with Judith Gershner.

And OK, just once. But STILL. I had NO IDEA she and my boyfriend had been . . . you know.

But I SHOULD have known. I mean, all the signs were there. That time she put her arm around his chair. And ate his garlic bread. I can't believe I was so blind.

I can't believe Michael wasted his Precious Gift on HER when he didn't even LOVE her.

WHAT IS WRONG WITH BOYS????

Uh-oh. Someone is texting me on my cell. This is just –

Oh. It's Tina.

Tina: Mia, where r u? What happened? Did
          u give him ur Precious Gift? Is he
          still going to Japan? Text me back!

I HAVE to text her back. I HAVE to tell her what's going on.

Mia: He said he was going to Japan
          whether we Did It or not. And

```
            Michael already gave his Precious
            Gift to Judith Gershner!!!!!
```

Tina: !!!!!!!!!!!!!!!!!

Thank God for Tina. I love her so much.

Mia: I NO!!!!!!!

Tina: BUT HE DIDN'T LUV HER!!!!!!!!!!!

Mia: He said it didn't mean anything,
            they were just 'messing around'.
            Tina, what am I going 2 do??????
            How could he not have told me?????

Tina: But he DID tell u.

Mia: A little late!!!!!

Tina: But he TOLD u.

Mia: HE DIDN'T EVEN LOVE HER!!!!!!!!

Tina: Lots of times in romance novels the
            hero has had meaningless sex with
            women b4 he meets the heroine.

Mia: WITH JUDITH GERSHNER?????

Tina: Well, no. But it just makes it MORE
            meaningful when he and the heroine

154

finally Do It. Bcuz sex is so much better when u luv the person.

Mia: I CAN'T BLIEVE U R DEFENDING HIM!!!! He said he was going to Japan even if we DID IT!!!!

Tina: I think u r right to b mad. But did u really break up?????

Mia: I gave him back his snowflake necklace.

Tina: MIA!!!!!!! NOOOOO!!!!!!!!!!!!!

Mia: TINA, HE LIED 2 ME!!!!

Tina: No, he didn't! He DID tell u. Eventually.

Mia: That is not the point. The point is JUDITH GERSHNER GOT 2 TOUCH IT B4 I DID!!!!

Tina: Lilly got 2 touch it b4 I did.

Mia: BUT SHE IS UR FRIEND!!!!! Besides, Boris and Lilly did not go ALL THE WAY. And Boris is not moving to Japan and leaving you alone for a year. Or MORE!!!!

Tina: True. Oh, Mia. I'm so sorry. I've

```
g2g, my dad says I've reached my
limit in text messages this month —
ttyl!
```

Tina's so sweet. She risked her dad's wrath to text me in my hour of need. She's a good and true friend.

Speaking of which . . . how am I ever going to face Lilly in the morning? I can't.

I just can't.

ME, A PRINCESS???? YEAH, RIGHT
A Screenplay by
Mia Thermopolis
(first draft)

Scene 24

INT/NIGHT – A large, comfortably furnished rent-controlled apartment on New York City's Fifth Avenue, off Union Square. A newly madeover MIA THERMOPOLIS has just entered through the front door. Her best friend, LILLY MOSCOVITZ, a slightly chubby, pug-faced girl, is staring at her incredulously.

> LILLY
>
> Oh my God, what happened to you?

> MIA
>
> (taking off her coat, trying to be casual)
> Yeah, well, my grandmother made me go see
> this guy Paolo, and he—

> LILLY
>
> (in state of shock)
> Your hair is the same colour as Lana
> Weinberger's. What's on your *fingers*?
> Are those fake fingernails? Lana has those
> too! Oh my God, Mia. You're turning into
> Lana Weinberger!

> MIA
>
> (unable to take it any more)
> Lilly, *shut up*.

MICHAEL
(appearing in the doorway with no shirt on)
Whoa.

LILLY
What? *What* did you just say to me?

MIA
You know what, Lilly? I'm a PRINCESS. I'm the
Princess of Genovia. And I will ALWAYS be a
princess, I can't escape it, I can't pretend
like it didn't happen. And as a princess, I will
always value princesslike qualities in other people,
such as honesty and self-respect and not Doing It
With People You Don't Even Love. Goodbye.

MICHAEL
Whoa.

MIA stomps from the room. LILLY and MICHAEL
exchange stunned glances.

Friday, September 10, 1 a.m., the Loft

Except of course I know now that the whole time –
maybe even way back when I was first finding out I'm a
princess – Michael was sleeping with Judith Gershner.

And I didn't know it.

Because he never told me.

Friday, September 10, 1.30 a.m., the Loft

HOW AM I GOING TO LIVE WITHOUT HIM?????

Friday, September 10, 2.15 a.m., the Loft

I have to be strong. I HAVE to. He LIED to me. He said maybe it was a good idea for us to TAKE A BREAK.

I can't just let him get away with that.

Maybe writing some poetry will help.

> You thought I gave you up for some
> Foolish feminist morals.
> You whose head ought to be wreathed
> In silver-plated laurels?
>
> For were you not a man?
> Was your sex not the best?
> Had you not a suit and tie,
> Big feet and hairy chest?
>
> Yet you opened up the cage
> For my headstrong reckless flight
> You thought I'd learn my lesson quick
> And return to you contrite.
>
> My freedom found, however,
> I disappeared from view.
> Maybe I'd catch no one nicer
> But anyone's better than you.
>
> Oh, our love affair was tragic!
> I wept with passionate strife.
> Till you let me go and I found out
> I prefer the single life.

God, I wish that were all true.

Michael! My cherished preserver!

161

Friday, September 10, 3 a.m., the Loft

Dear Michael,

I just wanted to say –

Dear Michael,

Why did you have to –

Dear Michael,

WHY????

Friday, September 10, 4 a.m., the Loft

Michael! My hope! My love! My life!

Friday, September 10, the limo on the way to school

I can't believe Mom made me go to school today.

I told her my heart was broken. I told her I hadn't slept A WINK ALL NIGHT LONG. I told her I can't stop crying. I haven't stopped crying since last night, practically. I had no idea human beings were even CAPABLE of producing so many tears.

It was like talking to a stone wall. Mom was all, 'You broke up with Michael, Mia, not the other way around. No way are you going to wallow around in bed all day.'

It's weird but . . . it's almost like she's on MICHAEL's side or something.

But that can't be possible, right? I mean, she's MY mom, not HIS.

Still. She even made ME call Lilly and tell her to find alternative transportation to school this morning. She refused to do it for me, even though I begged, because I was afraid Michael might see it was me on the caller ID, and pick up instead.

I feel bad leaving Lilly in a lurch without a ride, but NO WAY can I face Michael this morning. And I know he will TOTALLY be waiting in front of their building for me, because he left me an email to that effect this morning, which said:

```
SkinnerBx: I still don't understand what I did
           wrong. How is my having slept with
           someone before I even knew you
           liked me a crime? I don't get it.
               I guess I can see why you're
           upset about the Japan thing, but I
           don't know how many times I have to
```

164

explain that one of the reasons I'm doing this is for US before it sinks in. Lilly said Boris said something about clarinettists at lunch the other day, so I guess that's where that came from, but I still don't understand it. If you want to see other people while I'm gone, I guess I'm fine with that. Maybe it would even be a good thing.

Look, we have to talk, OK? I'll be waiting with Lilly out front before school. Maybe we could grab a coffee?

I HAD to call Lilly (on her cell, so there was no chance of getting Michael by mistake) and be all, 'Lilly? I can't come pick you up today.'

'POG?' Lilly sounded suspicious. 'Is that you?'

'Y-yes,' I said.

'Wait – are you CRYING?'

'Y-yes,' I said. Because I was.

'WHAT is going on?' Lilly wanted to know. 'What did you do to my brother? I've never seen him like this. Did you really dump him? Because he says you did.'

'He – he –'

But it was hopeless. I couldn't speak. I was crying too hard.

'Jesus, Mia,' Lilly said, actually seeming concerned about me for once in her life. 'You sound even worse than he does. WHAT IS GOING ON?'

'I c-can't talk right now,' I said. Because I literally *couldn't talk*, I was crying so hard.

'Fine,' Lilly said. 'But, Mia . . . seriously, I don't know what this is about, but you're breaking his heart. The only reason I'm not coming over there and kicking your ass for it is because I can tell your heart isn't doing so well either. But seriously, you *have* to talk to him. Just *talk* to him. I'm sure whatever it is, you two can work it out, if you just TALK. OK?'

I couldn't reply though. I was crying too hard.

If I could have said something, though, I'd have said, 'It's too late, Lilly. There's nothing left to say.'

Because there isn't.

I miss him so much. And he hasn't even left yet.

Friday, September 10, Intro to Creative Writing

ME, A PRINCESS???? YEAH, RIGHT
A Screenplay by
Mia Thermopolis
(second draft)

Scene 12

INT/DAY – The Palm Court at the Plaza Hotel in New York City. A flat-chested girl with upside-down-Yield-sign-shaped hair (fourteen-year-old MIA THERMOPOLIS) is sitting at an ornately set table across from a bald man (her father, PRINCE PHILIPPE). We can tell by MIA's expression that her father is telling her something upsetting.

> PRINCE PHILIPPE
> You're not Mia Thermopolis any more, honey.

> MIA
> (blinking with astonishment)
> I'm not? Then who am I?

> PRINCE PHILIPPE
> You're Amelia Mignonette Grimaldi Thermopolis Renaldo, Princess of Genovia.

> MIA
> (getting up from the table, pulling an Uzi from her backpack)
> Dad, look out!

NINJAS descend from the ceiling on ropes. MIA kicks over the table, sending the tea things flying. Then she strafes the room with bullets from her Uzi. TOURISTS and WAITERS dive for cover. Her dad, terrified, ducks behind a potted plant. MIA throws down the Uzi, which has jammed, and kickboxes the NINJAS, dispatching them one by one, à la River in the movie *Serenity*.

Finally, the room is still, all NINJAS unconscious. One by one, the TOURISTS and WAITERS climb to their feet. One of them begins to clap, slowly. He is joined by everyone else. Soon, MIA is receiving a standing ovation for her bravery.

MIA walks up to PHILIPPE and sticks out her right hand to help him to his feet. He hesitantly takes it. She pulls him up.

> PRINCE PHILIPPE
> (gratefully)
> Mia – where did you learn to –

> MIA
> (matter-of-factly)
> I've been working as a highly trained
> demon-killer for the Vatican for years,
> Dad. Didn't you know?

> PRINCE PHILIPPE
> I didn't know. I was wrong about you, Mia.
> You're not just a princess.

> MIA
> No, Dad. No, I'm not.

F

Mia, while this is highly imaginative, in no way does it satisfy the assignment, which was to describe a beloved pet.

K. Martinez

Friday, September 10, English

Are you OK?

I guess so, Tina. Thanks.

You look kind of . . . pale. And your eyes are red.

Yeah. Well. I didn't get much sleep last night.

Have you spoken to him yet? Michael, I mean?

No. Not in person.

Hasn't he called? Or texted?

Well, yes. But I haven't written back. How can I, Tina? What is there to SAY?

True. But if he apologized, wouldn't you forgive him?

He's not going to apologize, Tina. He doesn't think he did anything wrong!!!

But this can't be IT. I mean, it can't be OVER between you two. You love each other too much!!!!!

Michael himself said – in one of the emails he sent – that maybe it's better this way. You know, that we see other people while he's gone.

HE SAID THAT?????

Well, he didn't say HE was going to see other people, but that it was OK with him if I wanted to.

Wait - he really SAID that?

Yes. He did. Well, he said he guessed it HAD to be OK.

Oh, Mia! I don't know how to say this but - do you think maybe Your Precious Gift is wrong? Because in my favourite romance novels - The Sheikh and the Virgin Secretary and The Sheikh and the Princess Bride - none of the sheikhs were virgins, and it all turned out OK for them and THEIR girl-friends.

I didn't want to write what I wrote next. Really. It HURT me to say it. But someone HAD to. Because Tina just can't live in Tinaland for the rest of her life. She just can't.

Tina. Those are BOOKS.

But Tina wasn't backing down.

Your Precious Gift is a BOOK. How come it's right and not the sheikh books?

Tina. None of the sheikhs in those books Did It with Judith Gershner and then LIED about it, OK? None of the sheikhs in those books invented a robotic sur-gical arm and is leaving for Japan for a year. Or more.

171

And if they were, they'd take their virgin secretary princess bride WITH THEM.

I know. I just think maybe you should give Michael another chance.

How can I do that? Every time I think about him now, all I can picture in my head is Judith Gershner with her tongue in his mouth. And that is the LEAST disgusting thing I picture the two of them doing.

Yes. I felt that way when I found out about Lilly and Boris. But it goes away after a while, Mia. Really. In a few days you won't see Judith Gershner in your head any more when you think about Michael.

Thanks, Tina. I see what you're saying. I really do. But the problem is, in a few days – no, in a few HOURS – Michael will be gone. Possibly forever!

Mia! Oh my gosh, I'm sorry! I didn't mean to make you cry!

It's not you, Tina. It's me. I just – I just –

Mia, it's OK. You don't have to write another word. I'll shut up now.

God. How can it have come to this – me sitting in English class, CRYING???
In a way I wish Michael WAS a sheikh, and I was his

virgin secretary or princess bride. I know it's not very feminist of me to think that.

But if he whisked me off to his tent in the desert instead of moving to Japan, at least I'd know he really cared.

Friday, September 10, French

Mia! Is it true?

Yes, Perin. It's true that Michael admitted he had sex with Judith Gershner and he's moving to Japan and he and I are broken up. I feel really terrible about it and I don't want to start crying in French so can we not talk about it?

Um, no. I meant is it true that you would know what to do if a tsunami hit New York City?

Oh. Yes, that's true too.

I'm sorry about you and Michael. I didn't know. So I guess you're single now?

I never thought of it before. But yeah I guess I am.

Want to sleep over tonight?

Oh, thanks for the invitation, Perin, but I think I'm just going to go home and go to bed. I'm not really doing all that great, to tell you the truth.

Ok. Well, feel better!

Thanks!

Qu'est-ce que c'est que le merite incroyable d'une femme? demandez-vous. Selon la chaîne douze, le mérite incroyable d'une femme est sa capacité de nourrir ses enfants. Une femme avec

174

une carrière? Ça c'est une femme qui n'adore pas ses enfants, ou son mari. Ce n'est pas une chrétienne! C'est une serveuse de diable!

Mes camarades et moi nous nous somme regardées les unes les autres. Nous avons changé de chaîne. Et juste à l'heure!

$116 + 75 =$ only 191!!!!!! I need nine more words!

Oh, wait . . . the title. AND MY NAME:
Une Emission Pleine d'Action
Par
Amelia Mignonette Grimaldi Renaldo Thermopolis

YES!!!!
At least SOMETHING is going my way today.

Friday, September 10, between French and Lunch

My cellphone just buzzed. Michael left the following text message:

Michael: At least let me come by and try
           to explain. Even though that won't
           be easy because I'm still not clear
           on what exactly I did that was so
           wrong.

What is he talking about, *come by and try to explain*? How can he come by and try to explain? I'm in SCHOOL.

And how can he still not know what he did wrong?????

Friday, September 10, Lunch

You know what? I don't care. LET them stare at me. This is the most delicious thing I've ever eaten in this cafeteria. If I'd known the cheeseburgers were this good, as a matter of fact I'd have started eating them a long time ago.

And you know what? I don't even care. I mean, I still feel bad for the animals and stuff.

But in a way it's like . . . well, tough luck for them. The world is an unfair place. Sometimes you're the windshield. Sometimes you're the bug.

That's from a song my mom likes.

If there is such a thing as reincarnation, I'll probably come back as a cow, and I'll spend my whole life in a tiny stall I can barely move around in, and eventually someone will come around and bonk me on the head and then skin me and make my skin into a leather miniskirt and the rest of me into hamburger, and a girl whose boyfriend gave his Precious Gift to Judith Gershner will eat me, and that will just be too bad for me. It's the circle of life, baby.

Wow. I guess I'm a total nihilist now.

Lilly seems to think so. And she can't seem to believe it.

'A burger?' She just kept staring at my tray. 'You're eating a CHEESEBURGER?'

'I don't care any more,' I said. Because it's true. I don't. About anything. Being a nihilist and all.

'You and my brother,' she said, 'get into one fight, and you break up with him and start eating meat? He's right. You HAVE lost your mind.'

I put my burger down at that one.

'He SAID that?' I demanded. I didn't care that we were having this discussion in front of the whole lunch crowd – J.P., Boris, Ling Su, Tina, Perin. Why should I? I don't care about anything any more. 'Michael said I've lost my mind?'

'Basically,' Lilly said. 'And the fact that you're sitting there eating a cheeseburger proves it. You haven't eaten meat since you were six years old!'

'Well maybe it's time I started,' I said. 'Maybe if I'd been getting more protein this whole time, I wouldn't have made so many boneheaded decisions.'

'Which one of your many are you referring to?' Lilly asked acidly.

'Hey, Lilly,' J.P. said, quietly but firmly. 'Cut it out.'

Lilly looked startled. She isn't used to J.P. butting in on her conversations with me. Because he's never done it before.

But it was too late. Because my eyes were already filling up with tears. Again.

I guess I'm not a nihilist after all.

'If he thinks I've lost my mind,' I said to Lilly, barely able to contain a sob, 'then he doesn't get it AT ALL. I HAVEN'T lost my mind. I just can't DEAL with it any more.'

'Deal with what?' Lilly wanted to know. 'Having a guy who loves you so much that while you were off in Genovia this summer, he invented this fantastic thing that could change the face of medical history as we know it, just so he could prove he was good enough to be with you, only to have you slap him in the face when he explained that in order to get the thing off the ground he has to go away for a while?'

I just glared at her, even though it was kind of hard to see her through my tears.

'That's not it,' I said, 'and you know it.'

'Oh, wait, I know. Is it because all these months he didn't tell you about something he KNEW you wouldn't understand and would go bananas over, because it is in your nature to go bananas over the littlest things, and he wanted to spare you?'

'What he did,' I said, a catch in my voice, 'wasn't LITTLE—'

'Oh, spare me,' Lilly spat. 'Tina told me about that stupid book her aunt gave her. Are you really so ignorant that you don't know that this whole "Precious Gift" crap started off as men's way of controlling females so that they could limit their number of sexual partners and therefore ensure the legitimacy of their own offspring?'

'Hold on,' I said, glaring at her. Which was hard to do, considering the tears that were causing my nose to feel prickly. 'There is NOTHING wrong with waiting to have sex until you can do it with someone you love.'

'Of course there's not,' Lilly said. 'You're totally entitled to that belief. But CONDEMNING someone who doesn't necessarily SHARE that belief? That's no better than those fundamentalist judges in Iran who condemn women to be buried up to their necks in sand and have rocks thrown at their heads. Because any way you look at it, that's YOU punishing someone for not sharing YOUR morals.'

The tears totally came with that one. I mean, seriously. Comparing ME to one of those evil fundamentalist judges?

But Lilly wouldn't let up.

'Why don't you just admit what this whole fight with

179

Michael is REALLY about, Mia?' she snarled. 'You're mad because Michael won't do what you want and stay in New York to be your little lapdog. Because he has a mind of his own and he wants to use it to make a LIFE of his own. THAT's what this is all about. And DON'T try to deny it.'

That's when J.P. got up, grabbed Lilly by the arm and said, 'Come on. We're going for a walk,' and dragged her out of the cafeteria.

And that's also when I started to cry in earnest. Not sobbing or anything. Just quietly weeping, over the remains of my burger.

Yes. I am a pathetic crying meat-eater now.

Boris patted me on the shoulder and said, 'Don't cry, Mia. I think you're doing the right thing. Long distance relationships never work. Better to make a clean break of it, like this.'

'Boris,' Tina said, sounding exasperated.

'No,' I said. 'He's right.'

Because he is.

I just wish he wasn't.

Also that I was dead.

I just went and got some bacon to put on my cheeseburger.

Friday, September 10, Gifted and Talented

I almost skipped this class. Partly because I felt really sick after the burger. I definitely shouldn't have added the bacon.

But also partly because I didn't want to see Lilly again. Especially without J.P. to rein her in.

But I didn't skip because I figured I'd just get in trouble. And a trip to Principal Gupta's office is the last thing I need.

Also, I got some Tums from the nurse, and that seemed to help.

I was glad I didn't skip when I walked into class. Glad because the first thing I saw when I walked in was Lilly, WEEPING.

I wasn't glad she was crying. I was glad because she so obviously needed me. I mean, something had Happened. Something BIG.

Boris was standing there next to her, looking alarmed. I think it's only natural that I assumed Lilly was crying because of something Boris said to her, since he flung me this totally panicky look when I walked in.

'What did you do to her?' I asked him, shocked. Because Boris can be a jerk sometimes. But he honestly doesn't MEAN to be. And he's got a lot less jerky since Tina started going out with him.

'She was like this when I came in,' Boris insisted. 'It wasn't me!'

'Lilly.' I couldn't imagine what could be the matter with her. Surely it couldn't have anything to do with me and Michael. *That* would never make Lilly cry. Hardly anything made Lilly cry. Except . . . I gasped. 'Did Lana

Weinberger decide to run for student council president after all?'

'No!' Lilly said scornfully, between sobs. 'God! Do you think I'd be crying over something like *that*?'

'Well.' I stared down at her blankly. 'What is it then?'

'I don't want to talk about it,' Lilly said.

But I noticed her gaze slide towards Boris. What's more important, Boris noticed it too.

And so – exercising a little of the tact Tina has so carefully taught him – Boris said, 'I guess I'll just go start practising now,' and went and let himself into the supply closet.

I said, 'OK, he's gone. Now tell me.'

Lilly took a deep, shuddering breath. Then, glancing around at everyone else in the room – all of whom immediately ducked their heads, pretending to be engrossed in their individual projects, something that NEVER happens unless Mrs Hill is in the room, which she most decidedly was not just then – Lilly whispered, 'J.P. just broke up with me.'

I stared at her in complete and utter astonishment. '*What?*'

'You heard me.' Lilly reached up and wiped her eyes with the back of her wrist, leaving a long black mascara stain on each side of her face. 'He dumped me.'

I pulled out the chair next to Lilly's just in time to collapse into it and not on to the floor.

'You're joking,' I said. Because it was the only thing I could think of to say.

But it was painfully clear by the way tears continued to stream from her eyes that she *wasn't* joking.

'But *why*?' I asked. '*When*?'

'Just now,' Lilly said. 'Outside on the front steps, next

to Joe.' Joe is the stone lion that flanks the stairs leading to the front doors of Albert Einstein High. 'He said he felt really bad, but that he doesn't feel the same way about me that I do about him. He said he values me as a friend, but that he's never l-loved me!'

I couldn't stop staring at her. Somehow, this was way more horrible than what Michael had done to me. I mean, Michael had had sex with Judith Gershner and lied to me about it and all.

But he had never said he didn't love me.

'Oh, Lilly,' I breathed. I forgot about being a nihilist. All I could think about was how much Lilly was hurting. 'Oh, Lilly. I'm so sorry.'

'So am I,' Lilly said, wiping her eyes again. 'Sorry I was such an *idiot* for not admitting to myself what I KNEW was going on sooner.'

I blinked at her. 'What do you mean?'

'Well, the very first time I told him that I loved him and all he said was "thank you"? I mean, I should have taken that as a sign that he didn't feel the same way about me as I did about him, right?'

'But we all just thought it was because he wasn't used to having a girl like him,' I said. 'Remember, Tina said—'

'Right, that he was like the Beast from *Beauty and the Beast*, unused to human love and uncertain how to react to it. Well, guess what? Tina was wrong. It wasn't that he didn't know how to react. He just didn't love me back, and he didn't want to hurt my feelings by telling me so. So he just led me on, all these months.'

I couldn't help sucking in my breath. 'Oh, Lilly,' I said. 'No! I mean, he must have thought maybe—'

'– that he'd grow to love me?' Lilly managed a bitter smile. 'Yeah, well, apparently it didn't work.'

'Oh, Lilly,' I said. I could have killed J.P. right then. I really could have. I couldn't believe he was putting her through this.

And to do it at school! Of all places! I mean, why couldn't he have waited until they were somewhere alone, like Ray's Pizza, and broken the news to her then, so she could cry in private? What's *wrong* with boys?

I'll kill him. Seriously. I'm going to kill him.

I didn't even realize I'd said the words out loud until Lilly reached out and grabbed my wrist and said, 'Mia. No. Don't.'

I looked at her, startled. 'Don't what?'

'Don't say anything to him about it. Really. It's my fault. I . . . I sort of knew all along that he didn't love me.'

'*What?*' I've heard about this before. When victims of rat-fink boyfriends blame themselves for what the loser himself did.

But I never thought LILLY, of all people, would be one of them.

'What are you *talking* about, you knew? Obviously you didn't know, Lilly, or you wouldn't have—'

'No, it's true,' Lilly said, her voice hoarse with tears. 'When he never said he loved me back, I suspected that there was something wrong. But I – well, like you said – I thought he might *learn* to love me. So I stayed with him, instead of breaking it off, like I should have. It's not his fault. He tried, Mia. He really did. It was actually really nice of him not to let it go further than it did. He could really have taken advantage. But he didn't.'

I couldn't help being all, 'So, wait. Does that mean that you two never—'

Lilly's eyes narrowed. 'Nice try, POG,' she said. 'I'm down, but I'm not out. We still have a presidential election to plan, you know.'

I dropped my head down to the top of the desk. 'Lilly,' I said. 'I can't. I just can't. Can't you see I'm broken?'

'Well, I'm broken too,' Lilly said defensively. 'And I'm still able to FUNCTION. A woman needs a man like a fish needs a bicycle.'

I really hate this expression. I bet fish would totally want bicycles, if they had legs.

Then, in a gentler voice, Lilly added, 'Look, POG, about you and my brother. I'm sorry.'

'Thanks,' I said. And though I thought I had finished crying when I left the cafeteria, all the tears came rushing back.

'But I don't get it,' Lilly said.

'Of course you don't get it,' I said miserably to the top of the desk. 'You're his sister. You're on his side.'

'I may be his sister,' Lilly said. 'But I'm your best friend too. And it just seems like such a stupid waste. I know you're mad at him, but really . . . what did he do that was so wrong? So he slept with Judith Gershner. Big deal. It's not like he did it WHILE you two were going out.'

'It IS a big deal,' I insisted. 'I just . . . I never thought Michael, of all people, would do something like that. Sleep with someone he didn't even love. And then LIE to me about it. And I KNOW you think that's just me inflicting my beliefs on to him. But I always just assumed he and I shared the same beliefs. And now I

185

find out he's more . . . well, he's more like *Josh Richter* than he is like me!'

'*Josh Richter*?' Lilly rolled her eyes. 'Oh, please. How is my brother REMOTELY like Josh Richter?'

'Because sleeping with a girl you don't even love . . . that's something Josh Richter does.'

'It's only a Josh Richter thing to do if the girl had a major crush on him and he used her and she got hurt.'

I lifted my head to stare at her. 'You mean like you and J.P.?' I asked, trying to sound as concerned as possible.

Lilly just glared at me though. 'Nice try, Mia,' she said. 'But I'm not falling for that one.'

Dang.

'Mia,' Lilly said. 'You can't get all bent out of shape over the fact that Michael has been with other girls before you. That's just STUPID.'

Now *I* narrowed my eyes at *her*. 'What do you mean, GIRLS?'

'Well, like that girl from Hebrew camp—'

'WHAT GIRL FROM HEBREW CAMP?' I screamed so loudly that Boris actually stuck his head out of the supply closet to see what was going on.

'Relax,' Lilly said disgustedly. 'They just made out. And he was like in ninth grade or something.'

'Was she pretty?' I wanted to know. 'Who was she? What base did they get to?'

'You,' Lilly said, 'need therapy. Now, can we talk about something other than our romantic travails for a moment? Because we need to work on your speech.'

I blinked at her. 'My what?'

'Your speech. You think just because we've broken up with our boyfriends, we're no longer capable of improving our academic environment or leading our peers to a better tomorrow?'

'No,' I said. 'But—'

'Good. Because you know you have to give your student-council-president speech at the assembly last period today, right?'

I swallowed. Hard. 'Lilly,' I said. 'That is not going to be possible.'

'You don't have a choice, POG,' Lilly said. 'I've let you off easy this week because of the whole Michael thing. But this part I can't do for you. You're going to have to get up there and speak. I figured you wouldn't have prepared anything, so I took the liberty of doing so.' She slid a piece of paper – covered with her tiniest handwriting – towards me. 'It's pretty much the answers to questions posed on the table-toppers in the caff. You know, what to do in the event of a Category Five hurricane or a dirty-bomb attack. Nothing new. At least, not to you. It should be a snap.'

'If I do this,' I asked in a sort of daze – maybe I was crashing from all the bacon – 'You'll tell me, right? If you and J.P. Did It over the summer?'

'Is that your sole motivation for running?' Lilly wanted to know.

'Yes,' I said.

'God, that is so pathetic. But yes, I will. You loser.'

I didn't take offence at this because she's right. I AM a loser. She doesn't even know how much.

Besides, I know that beneath Lilly's bravado she is clearly hurting inside. How could she not be? She adored J.P. in a way I've never seen her fall for any other guy.

Seriously, how could J.P. do this to her? I thought he was one of the good guys. I really did.

But now I honestly don't know how I'm going to be able to be friends with him. Let alone lab partners.

Friday, September 10, Chemistry

J.P. is acting like nothing happened! Like he thinks I don't know about him and Lilly! He asked, 'How are you, Mia?' when he sat down next to me, looking all concerned about me. Me! When *he's* the one who just stomped on my best friend's heart!

I was so shocked, I just went, 'Fine,' completely forgetting what I decided in the hallway on the way to class – that I am never speaking to J.P. again.

And OK, it isn't his fault, necessarily, that he doesn't love Lilly. But he could have told her sooner – like way back in May when she first told him that she loved him – instead of stringing her along this whole time.

Oh . . . Kenny is passing me a note:

Mia – I was very sorry to hear about you and Michael breaking up. If there is anything I can do to help make you feel better, please let me know. Kenny ☺

Kenny is so sweet. I can't believe he doesn't have a girlfriend. Hey, maybe Lilly –

Well, OK. Probably not. He's not really her type, seeing as how he weighs less than she does.

Thanks, Kenny. Helping me make sense of all this Chemistry stuff is really all I can think of at the moment. I'm really grateful for all your help.

No problem, Mia! I'm always here for you. Maybe if you aren't doing anything tonight you could come over and I could help you understand Avogadro's number. Because

I noticed you looked kind of confused by that. Plus my mom just went to the butcher, so we have lots of bacon, which I hear you're eating now.

Aw. See? He's such a nice guy. He TOTALLY needs a girlfriend. Maybe he and Perin would get along???

Oh, thank you, Kenny, that's very sweet, but I can't tonight. I'm not really feeling up to understanding anybody's number yet.

Well, the invitation's open anytime! You really don't need to be intimidated by Chemistry. It's easy – so long as you pay attention.

Good to know! Thanks again.

Amazing.

Oh my God. J.P. just passed me a note! How COULD he? I mean, he has to know how upset I am with him right now. He knows Lilly has G and T with me after lunch. He has to know she told me what he did. How dare he pass me a note? How DARE he?

Well, I'm not writing back. I'm not. I'm keeping my eyes on the blackboard. Chemistry is important, you know. Even princesses have to know it. For some reason.

Still . . . what's he talking about? What's so amazing?

What's amazing?

I can't believe I did that! I can't believe I wrote back! What's WRONG with me?

> That you've only been single for what, sixteen hours? And the wolves are already out.

!!!! WHAT???? What is he talking about? Oh, wait, KENNY? Is J.P. insane?

Kenny's not a wolf! He's just trying to be nice.

> You go right on telling yourself that if it makes you feel better. How are you doing though, REALLY?

Ha! Well, he asked for it:

How am I doing? I'll tell you how I'm doing. I was doing a lot better before you broke up with my best friend!!!!

Let's see how he responds to THAT.

> Oh. She told you.

Of course she told me!!!! What do you think???? Lilly and I tell each other everything. Well, ALMOST everything. J.P., how could you do that to her?

> I'm sorry. I didn't want to. I like Lilly, I really do. Just not the same way she likes me.

She didn't just LIKE you, she LOVED you. She told you that back in May. If you knew you didn't love her,

191

why didn't you tell her then? Why did you have to string her along for so long?

> Honestly, I don't know. I guess I hoped my feelings would change. But they never did. And today, when I saw how she treated you - well, I realized they never would.

How she treated me? What are you TALKING about?

> She was so mean to you at lunch. About what happened between you and Michael.

What???? Lilly wasn't mean to me!!!

> Mia, she equated your breaking up with Michael for lying to you with fundamentalist judges in Iran who order adulterous women to be stoned to death.

Oh, THAT. But that was just Lilly being . . . LILLY. I mean, that's just how she is.

> Well, that's not someone I want to be with. That shows a lack of compassion I frankly find unforgivable.

Wait . . . so you're saying you broke up with Lilly because of ME???

> Well . . . partly. Yes.

Oh, great. This is just GREAT. Like things aren't going

badly enough. Now I also have to shoulder the burden of responsibility for Lilly's broken heart?

J.P., that's just how Lilly IS. I'm USED to it. It doesn't bother me.

> But it SHOULD bother you. You deserve to be treated better. I think you let people treat you badly too often. You dismiss it as 'that's just how that person is'. But that doesn't make their behaviour right, Mia. That's why I think your taking a stand against Michael for what he did is a real step forward for you.

What is he TALKING about?

I don't let people treat me badly! I totally broke Lana's cellphone that one time . . . well, you weren't there. But I did.

> I'm not saying you NEVER stick up for yourself. I'm just saying it seems to take a lot to finally get a rise out of you. You tend to think the best of people — like Kenny and his blatant attempt to lure you into his clutches when you've been single less than twenty-four hours.

!

I told you! Kenny only thinks of me as a friend!

> Right. You go right on telling yourself that. I'm just glad you finally stuck up for yourself where Michael

193

is concerned. I like Michael, but it was wrong of him to lie to you about his sexual history. I think honesty is the most important thing in a relation-ship. And if Michael couldn't be honest with you about something as basic as who he has been with before you, what chance did you two really have at anything long-term?

Wow! FINALLY someone who gets it! Maybe J.P. isn't that bad after all. I mean, it's true he dumped Lilly – and at SCHOOL, of all places.

But he seems to really have his priorities straight.

I just hope that you and I can still be friends. I wouldn't want you to hold my breaking up with Lilly against me. I would hate for that to affect OUR friendship. Because I do consider you a close friend, Mia . . . one of the best I've ever had.

Oh my gosh! That is so sweet!

Thanks, J.P.! I think of you that way, as well. I can't tell you how much it means to me that you're on my side in all this, and not Michael's. So many boys WOULD take his side, I think. They just don't seem to understand that your virginity is the most precious gift you have to give to your one true love. If you waste it on someone you don't even care about, then you have nothing to give the person you DO care about when the time comes.

Exactly. That's why I've hung on to mine.

!!!! J.P. is a virgin!!!!!

Wow. He and I really DO have a lot in common.

Also . . . this means that Tina is wrong: J.P. and Lilly never Did It!!!!!!!!!!!

I'm not going to tell Lilly I know the truth though. She's had enough disappointments for one day. I'll let her have the fun of stringing me along for a bit longer. It's the least I can do, considering it's MY fault she and J.P. broke up.

I just really hope she never realizes this.

Friday, September 10, Pre-Calc

Oh my God, oh my God, oh my God. Did what just happened really happen? Or did I just imagine it?

It CAN'T have happened. Because it's too weird to actually have taken place.

Except . . . except I think it really did!

I'm going to throw up. I really am. *Why* did I eat that bacon cheeseburger for lunch?

My fingers are trembling so much I can barely write this . . . but I have to get it down somehow . . . OK, here goes:

Now I know what Michael meant when he said he was going to *come by and try to explain*. He meant he was going to come to ALBERT EINSTEIN HIGH SCHOOL.

And walk up to the door to seventh-period Chemistry just as I was coming out with J.P. Only at first I didn't notice him. Michael, I mean.

At least, not until after J.P. – who I'm sure hadn't noticed Michael either – went, 'Friends?' to me, and I said, 'Of course!'

And then he said, 'Hug?' And I was like, 'Why not?' And gave him one.

And I was so – I don't know – MOVED by how sad J.P. was, on account of breaking up with Lilly and all, that the next thing I knew, I was KISSING J.P.

I only meant to kiss him on the cheek. But he moved his head. And so I ended up kissing him on the lips.

Not like French or anything. And only for a second.

Still. I kissed him. On the lips.

It wouldn't have been any big deal – I'm sure it wouldn't – if it hadn't been for the fact that when I took my arms down from around his neck and turned around (all embarrassed, because I hadn't MEANT to kiss him. Or at least, not exactly) there was Michael.

Just standing there in the middle of the crowded hallway, looking stunned.

So many things went through my head when I turned around and saw Michael standing there, staring at me. Happiness at first, because I'm always happy when I see Michael. Then pain, when I remembered what he did to me and how we're broken up now. Then bewilderment, over what on earth he was doing at a school he already graduated from.

Then I realized he was there to *try to explain*, like he'd texted.

And then I saw his expression, and saw his gaze dart from my face to J.P.'s – poor J.P., who was standing there still as a statue, the hand he'd put around my waist when I'd stood on my tiptoes to kiss him still up in the air, like he'd forgotten how to move or something! – and back again.

And I knew EXACTLY what he was thinking.

Then all I felt was confused. Because Michael had to think – well, that there was something going on between me and J.P.

But it wasn't true, of course.

'Michael,' I said.

But it was too late. Because he was already *turning around and walking away*.

Walking away, like he'd suddenly realized he'd made a huge, colossal mistake in coming to see me at all!

I couldn't believe it! Apparently, I don't even mean enough to him to stay and try to hash it out with me! He didn't even stay to punch J.P. in the face for scamming on his girl!

I guess because I'm not actually his girl any more.

Also, I guess I shouldn't have been too surprised. I mean, when Michael saw me sexy dancing with J.P. at that party he had last year, he never said anything about it.

But he hadn't completely ignored me altogether afterwards either, like he's doing now.

Oh, God. I can't even think about it. I thought writing about it would help, but it hasn't. My fingers are STILL shaking as I write this. What's happening to me? My stomach is really upset too. It can't be the cheeseburger, that was hours ago . . . plus the nurse gave me those antacids . . .

WHY didn't he SAY ANYTHING? I WAS KISSING ANOTHER MAN. You'd have thought he'd at least have said SOMETHING, even if it was only, 'Goodbye, forever.'

Goodbye, forever. Oh, God. He's leaving tonight. Forever.

And he looked so GOOD standing there, so tall and strong, with his neck all freshly shaved (I think. I didn't exactly get an opportunity to go up to it and check. Or take a sniff. Oh, God! How I miss the smell of Michael's neck! If I smelt it right now, I bet I'd stop shaking and my stomach would stop rolling around).

He looked so shocked – so hurt –

Oh, God. I think I really am going to be sick . . .

Friday, September 10, the limo on the way to the Four Seasons

I was sick in the nurse's office. Lars got me there just in time.

I don't know what came over me. I was just sitting there in Pre-Calc, writing in my journal, and all of a sudden I pictured the shocked expression on Michael's face when I turned around from kissing J.P., and I started feeling sweaty all over, and Lars, who was sitting next to me, went, 'Princess? Are you all right?' in alarm, and I said, 'No,' and the next thing I knew, Lars had me by the arm and out the door and over the sink in the nurse's office, where I threw up what looked like the entire bacon cheeseburger I scarfed down at lunch.

Nurse Lloyd took my temperature and said it was normal but that there's a stomach flu going around, and that I probably have it. She said I couldn't stay at school or I'd infect everyone.

So she called the Loft, but no one was there. I could have told her that. Fridays this semester Mr G only has a half day, so he went home early. He and Mom probably headed out to New Jersey to catch whatever was showing at the five-dollar matinee, then stopped at Sam's Club to stock up on diapers for Rocky, their half-day tradition.

So Lars decided to take me to Grandmere's, since he didn't think I should be alone in the Loft in my current state.

Apparently being ill in the company of Grandmere is preferable to being ill in my own comfy bed. I fail to see the logic in this, but I was too weak to protest.

199

I didn't have the heart to tell Nurse Lloyd that what I have isn't the flu. What I have is Too-much-meat-after-a-lifetime-of-abstaining-from-it and My-boyfriend-gave-his-Precious-Gift-to-someone-else-and-is-moving-to-Japan-tonight.

But, just like with the flu, there's no pill you can take to make that go away.

Especially when it's accompanied by I-just-kissed-my-best-friend's-ex-boyfriend-and-*my*-ex-boyfriend-saw-me-do-it.

The saddest part of all is that the first person I wanted to call when I realized I was being booted out of school on account of being sick was . . . Michael. Because even just talking to Michael has always made me feel better.

But I can't call him. I can never call him again. Because what would I even SAY to him, after what just happened?

It's a really good thing this limo comes with its own barf bags.

Friday, September 10, 3 p.m., the Four Seasons

Grandmere is the worst person to hang around with when you aren't feeling well. Being a Cylon, she of course never feels sick – or at least, never remembers what it was like when she DID feel sick – and is completely lacking in compassion for anyone feeling out of sorts.

Worse, she is WAY excited that Michael and I broke up.

'I always knew That Boy was trouble,' she said all happily, when I explained what I was doing, showing up at her suite mid-afternoon, supposedly infected with a highly contagious disease. *I'm not sick, Grandmere*, I'd said. *I'm just sad.*

Because the problem is, I haven't stopped loving Michael. So instead of agreeing with her that he was trouble, I was just like, 'You don't know what you're talking about,' and went and sat on her couch, pulling Rommel on to my lap for comfort.

Yes. That's how far gone I was. I was looking to ROMMEL, a miniature poodle, for comfort.

'Oh, there's nothing inherently WRONG with Michael,' Grandmere went on. 'Except that he's a commoner. Well, tell me. What did he do? It must have been something particularly heinous, for you to have taken off That Necklace.'

My hand went to the empty spot at my throat. My necklace! I hadn't even realized how much I'd been missing it – how strange it felt not to have it on – until just then. Michael's necklace had been a bit of a bone of contention between Grandmere and me. She always wanted me to put on the Genovian royal jewels for balls and functions I attended, but I would never take Michael's necklace off, and let's just say Grandmere isn't a fan of the layered-necklace look.

Well, I guess a silver snowflake on a chain doesn't exactly go with a diamond and sapphire choker.

I figured there was no point in hiding the truth from Grandmere, since she'd weasel it out of me somehow. So I went, 'He slept with Judith Gershner.'

Grandmere looked delighted. Well, she WOULD.

'Cheated on you! Well, never mind. Plenty of fish in the sea. What about that nice boy who was in my play, the Reynolds-Abernathy boy? He'd make a lovely consort for you. Such a nice young man. So tall and blond and handsome!'

I just ignored that. What could I have said in reply? Sometimes I wonder if lunacy runs in the family.

Actually, I KNOW it does.

Instead, I said, 'Michael didn't cheat on me. He slept with Judith Gershner before we started going out.'

'Is she that horsefly girl?' Grandmere wanted to know. 'I can see why you'd be upset about, that. Those horrible black tennis shoes!'

'Grandmere.' Seriously. What is WRONG with her? 'It's not about how she LOOKS. It's that Michael LIED to me about it. I asked him if they were going out, and he said no. Plus, he didn't even LOVE her. What kind of person gives his Precious Gift to someone he doesn't even LOVE?'

Grandmere just looked at me. She seemed confused. 'His precious what?'

'GIFT.' God, she can be so dense. 'HIS PRECIOUS GIFT. You only have ONE. And he gave his to JUDITH

GERSHNER, a girl he didn't even CARE about. He should have waited. He should have given it to ME.'

I didn't mention the part about how he'd just caught me kissing another boy. Because it didn't really seem to pertain to the matter in hand.

Grandmere just looked more confused. 'Was this gift some kind of family heirloom? Because the rules of etiquette dictate that when a young man gives you a family heirloom, it is only yours to keep for the duration of the relationship and must be returned in the event of the dissolution of the engagement.'

'His Precious Gift isn't a RING, Grandmere,' I said, fighting for patience. 'His Precious Gift is his VIRGINITY.'

Grandmere blinked at me. 'His *virginity*? Virginity is no GIFT. You can't even WEAR it!'

'Grandmere,' I said. I can't believe she is so behind the times. Well, it's not surprising she has no idea what I'm talking about. I was listening to 'Dance, Dance' on my iPod the other day and she overheard it and said it was 'catchy' and asked who sang it and when I said Fall Out Boy, she accused me of lying and said no one would name a band something that stupid. I tried to explain that the name came from Bart Simpson, and she was just like, 'BART WHO? Do you mean WALLIS SIMPSON, that dreadful wife of the Duke of Windsor? She didn't have a relative named Bart. That I know of.'

See? She's hopeless.

'Your virginity is a Precious Gift you are supposed to give only to a person whom you love,' I explained slowly, so she'd understand. 'Only Michael gave his to Judith Gershner, a girl he didn't love and with whom, in fact, he says he was only "messing around". So now he has no gift to give me, the girl he professes to love, because he SQUANDERED his gift on someone he didn't even care about.'

Grandmere shook her head. 'That Miss Gershner did you a FAVOUR, young lady. You should be kissing her feet. No woman wants an inexperienced lover. Well, except apparently all these young, blonde female teachers I keep seeing on the news, who are sleeping with their fourteen-year-old male students. But I must say, they all appear to be mentally unhinged to me. What on earth do they TALK to these young boys about? Because it certainly isn't why their trousers are falling down. Tell me, Amelia, why IS that considered so fashionable? What is so appealing about a young man whose trousers are halfway down to his knees?'

I could think of no reply to this. Because what can you even SAY to that?

'In any case,' Grandmere went on, not even noticing I hadn't said anything. 'Isn't That Boy moving to Japan anyway?'

'Yes,' I said. And as usual my heart twisted at the sound of the word Japan. Just proving that

a) I still have a heart, and
b) I still love Michael, despite all my efforts not to. I mean, how could I not?

'Well, what does it matter, then?' Grandmere asked cheerfully. 'You'll probably never see him again.'

That's when I burst into tears.

Grandmere was pretty alarmed at this development. I mean, I was just sitting there, wailing. Even Rommel put his ears back and started whining. I don't know what would have happened if my dad hadn't walked in just then.

'Mia!' he said when he saw me. 'What are you doing here so early? And what's the matter? Why on earth are you crying?'

But I just shook my head. On account of how I couldn't stop crying.

'She broke up with That Boy,' Grandmere had to shout, in order to be heard over my sobs. 'I don't know what she's carrying on that way for. I told her it's all for the best. She'd be much better off with the Reynolds-Abernathy boy. Such a tall, handsome young man! And his father's so rich!'

This just made me cry harder, remembering how I'd kissed J.P. in the hallway, right in front of Michael. I hadn't meant to, of course – but what did that matter? The damage was done. Michael was never going to speak to me again. I just knew it.

The fact that I so desperately wanted him to, in spite of everything that had happened between us, was what was making me cry hardest of all.

'I think I know what she needs,' Grandmere went on as I continued to wail.

'Her mother?' Dad asked hopefully.

Grandmere shook her head. 'Bourbon. Does the trick every time.'

Dad frowned. 'I think not. But you might have your maid ring for some hot tea. Maybe that will help.'

Grandmere didn't look very hopeful, but she went off to get Jeanne to ring for tea, while Dad stood there, looking down at me. My dad's not really used to seeing me cry like that. I mean, I've cried in front of him plenty of times – most recently over the summer when we were at a state function at the palace and I walked into a low-hanging roof-beam while wearing my tiara and the combs dug into my head like tiny knives.

But he is not used to me having dramatic emotional outbursts, because despite the ups and downs of the past few years things have been going fairly well and I have been able to keep it together.

Until now.

I just kept on bawling, and reaching for tissues from the box on the table by the couch. In between wails it all kind of poured out, about the Precious Gift and Judith Gershner and the snowflake necklace and how Michael had come to school to see me and instead saw me kissing J.P.

I have to admit, Dad looked pretty stunned. I don't really talk about, you know, sex, with my dad, because, um, ew.

And I could tell the Precious Gift thing was freaking him out, because he sank down on to the end of the couch like he had kind of lost the ability to stand up. And he just sat there listening to me until I finally wound down and couldn't talk any more and was just sitting there, blowing my nose, the worst of the tears over.

God, I had no idea human beings even had the ability to produce so many tears.

Only when I'd cleaned up most of the snot from my face did Dad think of something to say. And when he did, it was NOT what I was expecting.

'Mia,' Dad said sombrely. 'I think you're making a mistake.'

I couldn't believe it! I'd basically just told him that Michael is a man slut! You would think my own father would want me to stay far away from a man slut! What was he TALKING about, a mistake?

'True romantic love really doesn't come around that often,' he went on. 'When it does, it's foolish to throw it away because of some silly thing the object of your affections did before the two of you were even dating.'

I just stared at him. I don't think it was my imagination that he looked so much like the elf king in *The Lord of the Rings*.

If the elf king had been totally bald, I mean.

'It's even more foolish to let someone you feel that strongly about go – at least, not without a fight. That's something I did once,' Dad went on, after clearing his throat. 'And I've always regretted it, because the truth is I've never met anyone I felt that way about ever again. I don't want to see you make the same mistake, Mia. So think – really *think* – about what you're doing. I wish I had.'

Then he got up to go answer the phone, which had started ringing.

I just sat there, completely stunned. Was that speech supposed to have HELPED me? Because it so didn't.

Dad should have just got Lars to shoot me. That's the only way I'll ever be put out of this misery.

Friday, September 10, the Four Seasons

The tea is here. Grandmere is making me pour. She is going on about some argument she once had with Elizabeth Taylor about whether or not pantsuits are proper attire for women attending afternoon tea. Elizabeth Taylor thinks they are. Grandmere thinks not (no surprise there).

Something is bothering me. I mean something besides the fact that my boyfriend and I have broken up because he slept with Judith Gershner, and that an hour or so ago he caught me making out (well, sort of) with my best friend's ex-boyfriend.

I can't stop thinking about Dad's little speech. You know, the one about how he once let someone he cared about go without a fight. He'd just looked so . . . sad.

And my dad is not really a sad sort of guy. I mean, would YOU be sad, if you were a prince and had Gisele Bundchen's private cellphone number?

Which is why I interrupted Grandmere's tirade against pantsuits to ask if she knew who Dad was talking about.

'Someone he cared about and let go without a fight?' Grandmere looked thoughtful. 'Hmmm. It could have been that housewife woman . . .'

'Grandmere,' I said. 'That thing in *Us Weekly* about Dad dating Eva Longoria was just a rumour.'

'Oh. Well, then I have no idea. The only woman I've ever known him to mention more than once is your mother. And that, of course, is because she's your mother. If it weren't for you, of course, he'd never have seen her again, once she turned down his proposal. Which, of course, was the stupidest mistake SHE ever made. Saying no, to a prince? Pfuit! Of course, it was a good thing in the end. Your mother would never have fitted in at the palace. Pass the Sweet 'n Low, please, Amelia.'

God. That is so weird. Who could it have been, then? I mean, who could my dad have cared about that he let walk away? Who –

Friday, September 10, the steps outside the Four Seasons

I can't believe this. How stupid I've been, I mean.

Dad tried to tell me. EVERYONE tried to tell me. But I was just so STUPID –

But I can fix this. I KNOW I can. I just have to get to him before he gets on the plane, and I'll tell him –

Well, I don't know what I'll tell him. But I'll figure it out when I see him. If I can just smell his neck one more time, I know – I KNOW – everything will be all right.

And that I'll know what to tell him when I see him.

IF I can get to him before he gets on the plane. Because it's the middle of the afternoon and my dad's got the limo over at the UN which means Lars and I have to take a cab, only we can't find one because they all seem to have disappeared, which is ALWAYS what happens when you really need one, which is why shows like *Sex and the City* can be so bogus sometimes, because those girls ALWAYS get a cab, and the fact is, there are just way more people who need cabs than there are cabs and . . .

WHAT AM I GOING TO SAY TO HIM????

God, I can't believe how stupid I've been. How stupid and blind and dumb and ignorant and judgmental and WHAT DOES IT MATTER???? Seriously, what does any of it MATTER, when I love him, and I'll never love anyone else, and it's not like he cheated on me and WHY AREN'T THERE ANY CABS????

I tore out of Grandmere's suite without even saying goodbye. I just yelled, 'We're leaving!' to Lars and bolted. He ran after me, looking confused. It wasn't until we ran into the lobby that I finally got Lilly on her cell and was like, 'WHAT AIRLINE?'

And Lilly was like, 'What are you talking about?'

'WHAT AIRLINE IS MICHAEL FLYING ON?' I screamed.

'Continental,' she said, sounding confused. 'Wait – Mia, where are you? We have assembly – you have to give your speech! Your speech for student-council president!'

'I can't,' I yelled. 'This is more important. Lilly, I have to see him –'

I was crying again. But I didn't even care. I've been crying so much, it's basically my natural state now. Which means maybe I'm not a nihilist after all. Because nihilists don't cry. 'Lilly. I just want to tell him – I just want to –' Except of course I still don't even KNOW what I want to tell him. 'Just tell me what time his plane is leaving – please?'

Something in my voice must have convinced her I was sincere.

'Six o'clock,' Lilly said, her tone softening. 'But he will already be at the airport. You have to check in like three hours early for international flights. Something I realize someone who only flies by Royal Genovian jet wouldn't know.'

So he was already at the airport. I hung up and ran outside and told Lars to flag down a cab.

Then I called my dad on his emergency number.

'Mia?' he whispered when he picked up. 'What is it? What's wrong?'

'Nothing's wrong,' I said. 'Was it Mom?'

'Nothing's wrong? Mia, this is my emergency line – I'm in the middle of the General Assembly – the

211

committee for disarmament and international security is speaking right now. I know you're going through a hard time dealing with the loss of your boyfriend, but unless you're actually bleeding, I'm hanging up.'

'Dad, don't! I need to know,' I said, urgently. 'The person you said you loved – the person you let go without a fight. Was it Mom?'

'What are you talking about?'

'WAS IT MOM? Was Mom the person you loved and regret letting go without a fight? It was, wasn't it? Because she said she never wanted to get married, and you HAD to get married in order to provide an heir to the throne. You didn't know you'd end up getting cancer and I'd be your only kid. And you didn't know you'd never meet anyone you loved as much as her. So you let her go without a fight, didn't you? It was her. It's *always* been HER.'

There was silence for a moment on my dad's end of the phone. Then he said, 'Don't tell her,' very quietly.

'I won't, Dad,' I said. I could barely see Lars out on the kerb with the Four Seasons doorman, both of them frantically waving their arm at cabs that were all currently filled with passengers, because of my tears. 'I promise. Just tell me one more thing.'

'Mia, I really have to go –'

'Did you ever used to smell her neck?'

'*What?*'

'Mom's neck. Dad, I have to know . . . Did you ever used to smell it? Did it smell really good to you?'

'Like freesias,' Dad said faintly. 'How did you know that? I've never told anyone that.'

Mom's neck smells nothing like freesias. Mom's neck

smells of Dove soap and turpentine. Oh, and coffee, because she drinks so much of it.

Except to Dad. Dad can't smell any of that. Because for him, Mom was the One.

Just like Michael is my One.

'Dad,' I said. 'I gotta go. Bye.'

I hung up just as Lars yelled, 'Princess! Here!'

A cab! At last! I'm saved!

Friday, September 10, cab on the way to John F. Kennedy International Airport

I don't believe this. It doesn't seem possible. But there's no mistake: We're in Ephraim Kleinschmidt's taxicab.

Yes. The same Ephraim Kleinschmidt in whose taxicab I wept so many bitter tears the other night.

Ephraim took one look at me in the rear-view mirror and went, 'YOU!'

Then he tried to hand me his Kleenex again.

'No Kleenex!' I yelled. 'JFK!!! Take us to JFK, as fast as you can!'

'JFK?' Ephraim balked. 'I'm about to go off duty!'

That's when Lars showed him his side arm. Well, really, he was just reaching for his wallet, saying there was an extra twenty in it if Ephraim got us to the airport in under twenty minutes.

But I'm pretty sure the Glock spoke more than the twenty.

Ephraim didn't hesitate. He put the pedal to the metal. Well, at least until we got to the first traffic light.

This is excruciating. We're never going to make it.

Except that we HAVE to. I can't let Michael go – not without a fight. I can't end up like my dad, with no one special in my life, dating supermodel after supermodel, because I allowed the person I really loved to slip through my fingers!

And sure, it's possible that when I get to the airport, Michael will be like, 'Get away.' Because, let's face it – I screwed up. Not that I didn't have a right to be hurt by what Michael did.

But I guess I should maybe have been a little bit more understanding and a little less judgmental.

Everyone TRIED to tell me. Mom. Tina. Lilly. Dad.

But I wouldn't listen.

Why didn't I listen?

And WHY did I kiss J.P.???? WHY WHY WHY?????

All I can do is try to explain. That it didn't mean anything – that J.P.'s just a friend. That I'm a horrible, terrible person, and that I deserve to be punished.

Only not by Michael's never speaking to me again. ANYTHING but that.

And even if Michael is like, 'Get away,' at least maybe I'll be able to sleep tonight. Because I'll have tried. I'll have *tried* to make things right.

And maybe just knowing I tried will be enough.

Lars was just like, 'Princess. I don't think we're going to make it.'

That's because we're currently stuck behind a stalled tractor-trailer on the bridge.

'Don't say that, Lars. We're going to make it. We HAVE to make it.'

'Maybe you should call him. To let him know we're on our way. So he doesn't go through security before we get there.'

'I can't CALL him.'

'Why not?'

'Because he'll never pick up if he sees it's me. After what he saw me do outside Chemistry?'

Lars raised his eyebrows. 'Oh,' he said. 'Right. I forgot about that. But what if he's already gone through security? You won't be able to get through without a ticket.'

'Then I'll buy a ticket.'

'To JAPAN? Princess, I don't think—'

'I won't actually GO to Japan,' I assured him. 'I'll just go to the gate to find him.'

'You know I can't let you go alone.'

'I'll buy a ticket for you too.' Fortunately I have my emergency-only Royal Genovian black American Express card on me. I've never actually used it before. But this IS what my dad gave it to me for: emergencies.

And this is an emergency, all right.

'I think you should just call him,' Lars said. 'He might pick up. You never know.'

I looked Lars dead in the eye. 'Would you?' I asked. 'If it were you?'

'Er,' he said. 'Well, no. Probably not.'

'Hey.' Ephraim Kleinschmidt glared at us in the rear view mirror. Ephraim had got out from behind the tractor-trailer and was making serious time along the highway now. 'I'm not turning around. We're almost there.'

'I'm not calling him, Lars,' I said. 'Not unless I have to. I mean, Arwen wouldn't *call* Aragorn.'

'Who?'

'Princess Arwen. She wouldn't *call* Aragorn. Something like this requires a BIG GESTURE, Lars. I'm no Arwen. I haven't saved any hobbits from peril or outraced any Ringwraiths. I already have a lot of strikes against me – I acted like a snotty jerk, I kissed another guy, AND I haven't made any particularly valuable contributions to society . . . not like Michael will, when his robotic surgical arm revolutionizes heart surgery as we know it. I'm just a princess.'

'Wasn't this Arwen just a princess?' Lars wanted to know.

'Yes. But her hair didn't look as stupid as mine does right now.'

Lars looked at my head. 'True.'

I couldn't even get offended. Because when you're already at rock bottom, nothing hurts any more.

'Plus,' I added, 'Arwen never tried to keep Aragorn from completing his quest, the way I tried to keep Michael from completing his. Arwen played a crucial role in the destruction of the One Ring. What have I ever done?'

'You built houses for the homeless,' Lars pointed out.

'Yeah, so did Michael.'

'You got parking meters installed in Genovia.'

'Big whoop.'

'You saved the Genovian bay from killer algae.'

'No one cares about that but the fishermen.'

'You got recycling bins installed all over the school.'

'And bankrupted the student government doing so. Face it, Lars: I'm no Melinda Gates – donating millions of dollars to help eradicate malaria, the biggest health crisis facing the globe, causing over a million children to die needlessly every year, just from the lack of a three-dollar mosquito net. I'm really going to have to start working on becoming something special if I'm going to hang on to Michael. I mean, if he'll even take me back after this.'

'I think Michael likes you the way you are,' Lars said, grabbing the handle of the door to keep from sliding over and crushing me as Ephraim Kleinschmidt swerved into the exit lane.

'He DID,' I said. 'Before I blew it by dumping him. And kissing his sister's ex-boyfriend right in front of him.'

'True,' Lars said.

Which is, in a way, one of the reasons I love Lars so much. You don't have to worry about him saying anything just to make you feel better. He always tells the truth. As he sees the truth, anyway.

'What airline?' Ephraim Kleinschmidt wanted to know.

'Continental,' I said. I had to hang on to the safety strap to keep from being hurled from one side to the other of the back seat. 'Departures!'

Ephraim put his foot on the accelerator.

Can't write any more. Fear for my life.

Friday, September 10, JFK International Airport, limo shelter

Well. That really didn't work out the way I'd hoped it would.

I'd really hoped that what would happen was, I'd walk into the airport and see Michael standing in the security line. I would call his name and he would turn around and see me, and duck out of the security line and come over, and I would tell him how sorry I was for being such a total ass, and he would forgive me instantly and wrap me in his arms and kiss me and I would smell his neck and he would be so moved he'd decide to stay in New York.

Well, I wasn't actually hoping for that last part. Well, I mean, of course I WAS. But I didn't really think it would HAPPEN. I would have settled for just his forgiving me.

But it turned out none of it happened. Because Michael's flight was taking off as we got to the ticket counter.

We were too late.

I was too late.

Now Michael's gone. He's on his way to another country – another CONTINENT – another HEMISPHERE.

And I'll probably never see him again.

Of course I did the only sensible thing I could, under the circumstances: I sat down on the airport floor and cried.

Lars had to half drag, half carry me to the limo stand, where we're waiting for Hans and my dad to come pick us up. Because Lars says over his dead body is he ever getting in another taxicab.

At least there's a bench here, so I can sit on it and cry, instead of the ground.

I just don't understand how any of this happened. A week ago – four days ago – I was so filled with hope and excitement. I didn't even know what pain was. Not real pain.

And now it's like my whole world has come collapsing down around my ears. And some of it I didn't have anything to do with – like Michael's decision to go to Japan.

But a lot of it is my own fault.

And for what?

How am I going to go on without him? Seriously?

Oh. The limo's here.

I'm going to see if we can go to the McDonald's drive-through on the way home. Because I think the only thing that might make me feel even slightly better is a Quarter Pounder.

With cheese.

Friday, September 10, 7 p.m., the Loft

When I got home, Mom and Mr G were just getting ready to order dinner. Mom took one look at me and was like, 'Bedroom. *Now*,' because Rocky had pulled all the pots and pans from the kitchen cupboards and was banging on them (a trait he no doubt inherited from his father, whose drum set still has a prominent place in our living room).

So I dragged myself into my bedroom and collapsed on to my bed, startling Fat Louie, who was so surprised when I landed on him, he actually hissed at me.

But I didn't care. I think I have dysthymia, or chronic depression, since I have all the symptoms:

– Emotional numbness
– Perpetual, low-level melancholy
– Feeling of merely going through the motions of everyday life with very little enthusiasm or interest
– Negative thinking
– Anhedonic (unable to savour or enjoy anything)

'Your father tells me you were sent home from school in the middle of the afternoon,' Mom said after shutting the door, so that the sound of at least some of the banging was lessened. 'And I understand from Lars that you went to the airport to try to say goodbye to Michael.'

'Yeah,' I said. Seriously, I have zero privacy. I can't do ANYTHING without the whole world finding out about it. I don't know why I even try to keep anything secret. 'I did.'

'I think that was the right thing to do,' Mom said. 'I'm proud of you.'

I just stared at her. 'I missed him. His flight had left already.'

Mom winced. 'Oh. Well. You can still call him.'

'Mom,' I said. 'I can't call him.'

'Don't be silly. Of course you can.'

'Mom. I can't call him. I kissed J.P. And Michael saw me do it.'

Now it was Mom's turn to stare at me. 'You kissed your best friend's boyfriend?'

'Actually,' I said, 'Lilly and J.P. broke up today. So he's her ex-boyfriend. But yes.'

'And you did this in front of Michael.'

'Yes.' I'm not sure the Quarter Pounder with cheese was actually the best idea. 'I didn't mean to though. It just sort of . . . happened.'

'Oh, Mia,' Mom said with a sigh. 'What am I going to do with you?'

'I don't know,' I said, tears tickling my nose. 'I've completely ruined everything with him. He'll never forgive me. He's probably glad to be rid of me. Who wants a crazy girlfriend?'

'You were crazy before Michael met you,' Mom said. 'It's not like you've got any noticeably crazier.'

The thing is, I knew she was *trying* to be encouraging.

'Thanks,' I said through my tears.

'Look,' she went on. 'Frank and I are ordering from Number One Noodle Son. Do you want anything?'

I thought about it. The Quarter Pounder really wasn't sitting all that well. Maybe what I needed was some more protein, to help keep it down.

'I guess some General Tso's chicken,' I said. 'And orange beef. And maybe some fried dumplings. And how about some spare ribs? You guys always seem to look like you're really enjoying those.'

But my mom, instead of looking happy that she didn't have to order a vegetarian entrée that no one but me was going to eat, looked concerned.

'Mia,' she said. 'Are you really sure you want to –'

But I guess something in my face made her change her mind about finishing that statement, since she just shrugged and said, 'All right. Whatever you want. Oh, and Lilly called. She wants you to call her back. She said it's important.'

'OK,' I said. 'Thanks.'

Mom opened my bedroom door – BANG! Giggle. BANG! BANG! – and left. I stared at the ceiling for a while. On Michael's ceiling, in his bedroom back at the Moscovitzes' apartment, there are glow-in-the-dark constellations. I wondered if he'd put glow-in-the-dark constellations on the ceiling of his new bedroom. In Japan.

I leaned down and picked up the phone and dialled Lilly's number. Dr Moscovitz picked up. She said, 'Oh, hello, Mia,' in a not-very-warm voice.

Yes. My boyfriend's mother hates me now.

Well, she has a right to.

'Dr Moscovitz,' I said. 'I'm sorry about – well, everything. I'm a huge jerk. I understand if you hate me.'

Dr Moscovitz's voice warmed up a tiny bit.

'Oh, Mia,' she said. 'I could never hate you. Look, these things happen. I – well, you and Lilly will work it out.'

'Right,' I said, feeling fractionally better. Maybe I didn't have dysthymia after all. I mean, if I could actually feel something. Besides bad. 'Thanks.'

Except . . . did she say 'you and *Lilly*'? She must have meant 'you and Michael'.

'Um,' I said. 'Is Lilly there, Dr Moscovitz? I'm returning her call.'

'Of course, Mia,' Dr Moscovitz said. And she called for Lilly, who picked up the phone and said, without preamble, 'YOU KISSED MY BOYFRIEND????'

I stared at the phone, totally confused. 'What?'

'Kenny Showalter says he saw you kiss J.P. outside your Chemistry classroom today,' Lilly snarled.

Oh, God. Oh. My. God.

The Quarter Pounder with cheese moved up my throat a little more as complete and total panic gripped me.

'Lilly,' I said. 'It wasn't – Look. It wasn't what Kenny thinks—'

'So you're saying you DIDN'T kiss my boyfriend outside your Chemistry classroom?' Lilly demanded.

'N-no,' I stammered. 'I'm not. I did kiss him. But just as a friend. And besides, technically, J.P. is your EX-boyfriend.'

'You mean like you're *technically* my ex-best friend?'

I gasped. 'Lilly! Come on! I told you! J.P. and I are just friends!'

'What kind of friends KISS each other?' Lilly demanded. 'On the mouth?'

Oh my God.

'Lilly,' I said. 'Look. We've both had a really bad day. Let's not take it out on each other—'

'I haven't had a particularly bad day,' Lilly snapped. 'I mean, sure, my boyfriend dumped me. But I also got elected as the new student-council president of Albert Einstein High School.'

I actually sat up on hearing this. 'You DID?'

'That's right,' Lilly said, sounding very self-satisfied. 'When you ducked out of school on account of your little tummy ache, Principal Gupta said you disqualified yourself from the race.'

'Oh, Lilly,' I breathed. 'I'm so sorry.'

'Don't be,' Lilly said. 'I asked Principal Gupta what would happen if no one ran – you know, for the student council. And she said Mrs Hill would just have to preside over it. Well, you know how THAT would turn out: We'd be selling candles from here to Spring Break. So I asked Principal Gupta if I could run in your place, and she said, seeing as how there were no other candidates, she didn't see why not. So I gave your speech. You know, the one about all the things people should do in the event of catastrophes? I guess I embellished a bit. Nothing TOO much. Just, you know, a few bits about supervolcanoes and asteroids . . . nothing major. People were too afraid NOT to vote for me. They held the vote last period. And I won. Well, over fifty per cent, anyway. I KNEW this freshmen class would respond to fear and fear alone. It's all they've ever known, after all.'

'Wow,' I said. 'That's great, Lilly.'

'Thanks,' Lilly said. 'Although I don't know what I'm telling YOU for, since you didn't help in any way. You are not my vice-president, by the way. Perin is. I don't need a boyfriend stealer as my vice-president OR as a friend.'

'Lilly,' I said. 'I did NOT steal your boyfriend. I told you, I only kissed him because – well, I don't know why I kissed him. I just did. But—'

'You know what, Mia?' Lilly snapped. 'I don't want to hear it. Why don't you save it for someone who cares? Like J.P., for instance.'

'J.P. doesn't like me that way, Lilly,' I couldn't help snapping back. 'And you know it!'

'Do I?' Lilly asked with an evil laugh. 'Well, maybe I know something you don't know then.'

'What are you *talking* about?' I demanded. 'Come on, Lilly, this is stupid. We've been friends too long to let a GUY come between us—'

'Yeah?' Lilly said. 'Well, maybe we've been friends long enough then. Goodbye, POG.'

Then I heard a click. Lilly hung up on me.

I couldn't believe it. Lilly *hung up* on me.

I sat there, not having the slightest idea what to do. The truth was, I couldn't believe any of this was happening. I'd lost my boyfriend and my best friend all in the same week. Was such a thing even possible?

I was still sitting there, holding the phone, when it rang again. I was so sure it was Lilly calling back to apologize for hanging up on me that I answered on the first ring and said, 'Look, Lilly, I am so, so sorry. What can I do to make it up to you? I'll do ANYTHING.'

But it wasn't Lilly. A deep, masculine voice said, 'Mia?'

And my heart soared. It was Michael. MICHAEL WAS CALLING ME! I didn't know how, since he was supposedly on a plane. But what did I care? It was MICHAEL!

'Yes,' I said, my bones turning to jelly with relief. It was MICHAEL! I practically burst into tears – but this time with happiness, not sadness.

'It's me,' the voice said. 'J.P.'

My bones went from jelly to stone. My heart crashed back down to earth.

'Oh,' I said, desperately trying to keep my disappointment from sounding obvious. Because a princess should

226

always try to make callers feel welcome, even if they aren't the caller she was expecting. Or hoping for. 'Hi.'

'I take it you already talked to Lilly,' J.P. said.

'Um,' I said. How could I have thought it was Michael? Michael was on a plane, flying halfway across the world from me. And why would Michael ever bother calling me again, after what I did? 'Yeah. Yeah, I did.'

'I'm guessing it probably went about as well as when I tried to talk to her just now,' J.P. said.

'Yeah,' I said. I felt numb. Was numbness a symptom of dysthymia? Not just emotional numbness, but actual PHYSICAL numbness? 'She pretty much hates my guts. And I guess she has a right to. I don't know what I was thinking back there outside Chemistry, J.P. I am so, so sorry.'

J.P. laughed. 'You don't have to apologize to me,' he said. 'I thoroughly enjoyed it.'

It was nice of him to be so chivalrous about it. But it somehow made it a little worse, in a way.

'I'm such an idiot,' I said miserably.

'I don't think you're an idiot,' J.P. said. 'I just think you've had a really bad week. That's why I'm calling. I figured you'd need cheering up, and I think I've got just the ticket. Literally.'

'I don't know, J.P.,' I said dully. 'I think I have dysthymia.'

'I don't have the slightest idea what that is,' J.P. said. 'But I do know that I am holding in my hand two box-seat tickets to tonight's Broadway performance of *Beauty and the Beast*. Would you be interested in coming with me?'

I couldn't help gasping. Box seats, to my favourite musical of all time?

'H-how –' I stammered. 'How did you –'

'Easy,' J.P. said. 'My dad's a producer, remember? So. You up for it? Show starts in an hour.'

Was he *kidding*? How had he *known*? How had he known this was EXACTLY what I needed to get my mind off what a total and complete jerk I had been to the two people I cared about most in the world (besides Fat Louie and Rocky, of course)?

'I'm up for it,' I said. 'I'm totally up for it!'

'I'll meet you outside the theatre in forty-five minutes,' J.P. said. 'And, Mia.'

'What?'

'Just for tonight, let's not mention either of the Moscovitzes. Deal?'

'Deal,' I said, smiling for what felt like the first time all day. 'See you in a few minutes.'

I hung up the phone.

Then, before I went to change out of my school uniform and into something nice for the theatre, I got up and walked over to my computer.

I clicked on my email. No new messages.

But that was OK. I wasn't expecting any. I didn't actually *deserve* any.

I clicked on Michael's last email to me – the one I hadn't answered. Then I clicked REPLY.

Then I thought for a while.

Then, finally, in the blank space, I wrote:

Michael. I'm sorry.

Then I clicked SEND.

GALWAY COUNTY LIBRARIES

air head

meg cabot

She's a brainiac trapped inside the body of an airhead . . .

Teenagers Emerson Watts and Nikki Howard have nothing in common. Em's a tomboy-brainiac who couldn't care less about her looks. Nikki's a stunning supermodel; the world's most famous airhead. But a freak accident causes the girls' lives to collide in the most extraordinary way – and suddenly Em knows more about Nikki's life than the paparazzi ever have!

The first book in a spectacular, romantic NEW TRILOGY with a spine-tingling twist!

A selected list of titles available from Macmillan Children's Books

The prices shown below are correct at the time of going to press. However, Macmillan Publishers reserves the right to show new retail prices on covers, which may differ from those previously advertised.

All Pan Macmillan titles can be ordered from our website, www.panmacmillan.com, or from your local bookshop and are also available by post from:

Bookpost, PO Box 29, Douglas, Isle of Man IM99 1BQ
Credit cards accepted. For details:
Telephone: 01624 677237
Fax: 01624 670923
Email: bookshop@enterprise.net
www.bookpost.co.uk

Free postage and packing in the United Kingdom